"You don't h
poker to

Brady held up his hand. "Of course not. But you've got to give this a lot of thought."

"I have. I can learn it, and I can sure use the money."

There was something about Molly. Her determination impressed him even as it warned him about possible complications down the road. Maybe the bet was crazy, but the consequences were real enough.

He gave her a serious head-to-toe appraisal. She stared right back at him. She had guts. Her answers were quick and decisive. She was obviously ambitious and wasn't afraid of taking a risk. All good qualities in a poker player. Maybe this would work out. All he had to do was set some limits, let her know he was the boss.

She placed her hands on her hips. "I don't know what you're thinking about, Brady, but I've got to have an answer." Never flinching, she added, "I can do this. You won't be sorry. So what'll it be?"

Dear Reader,

The release of this book marks the end of one of the most fun and challenging experiences I've had as a writer When my editor invited me to participate in a continuity series starring five guys who play Texas Hold 'Em poker together, I jumped at the chance. Not only do I like watching Hold 'Em tournaments on TV, my husband is something of an expert at the game, and I enjoy playing myself. I couldn't wait to develop a hero who would match wits with a circle of buddies from all walks of life, and to lead this guy into a romantic entanglement that would take all five guys to figure out.

I learned a couple of important things about poker and friendships. Both require nurturing, patience and understanding. But the similarity ends there, because when the cards aren't falling the way you want them to, true friendships remain strong. I hope you'll come to appreciate what the support of each of these card-playing guys means to Brady as he makes the biggest gamble of his life by taking a chance on a girl and a horse.

And I hope you read the other four books in this series, each one unique because of what Tara Taylor Quinn, Debra Salonen, Linda Style and Linda Warren bring to the series. You'll meet five guys you won't soon forget. I know I'll never forget them.

I love to hear from readers. Please visit my Web site, www.cynthiathomason.com, e-mail me at cynthoma@aol.com or write to me at P.O. Box 550068, Fort Lauderdale, FL, 33355.

Sincerely,

Cynthia

Deal Me In

Cynthia Thomason

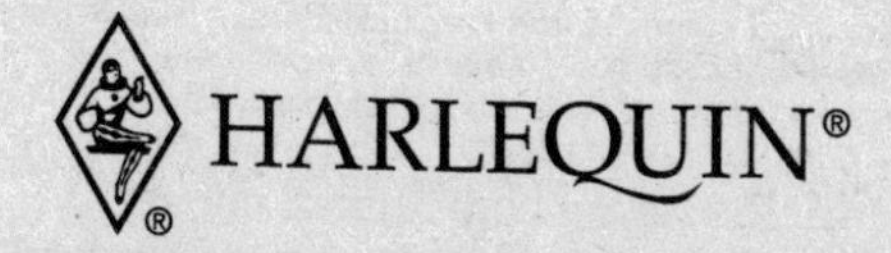

TORONTO • NEW YORK • LONDON
AMSTERDAM • PARIS • SYDNEY • HAMBURG
STOCKHOLM • ATHENS • TOKYO • MILAN • MADRID
PRAGUE • WARSAW • BUDAPEST • AUCKLAND

ISBN-13: 978-0-373-71464-3
ISBN-10: 0-373-71464-5

DEAL ME IN

This edition published by arrangement with Harlequin Books S.A.

www.eHarlequin.com

Printed in U.S.A.

ABOUT THE AUTHOR

Cynthia Thomason writes contemporary and historical romances and dabbles in mysteries. When she's not writing, she works as a licensed auctioneer in the auction business she and her husband own. In this capacity, she has come across scores of unusual items, many of which have found their way into her books. She loves traveling the U.S. and exploring out-of-the-way places. She has one son, an entertainment reporter, and an aging but still lovable Jack Russell terrier. Cynthia dreams of perching on a mountaintop in North Carolina every autumn to watch the leaves turn. You can learn more about her at www.cynthiathomason.com.

Books by Cynthia Thomason

HARLEQUIN SUPERROMANCE

1120–THE MEN OF THORNE ISLAND
1180–THE HUSBAND SHE NEVER KNEW
1232–THE WOMEN OF BAYBERRY COVE
1268–YOUR HOUSE OR MINE?
1312–AN UNLIKELY MATCH
1345–AN UNLIKELY FATHER
1393–AN UNLIKELY FAMILY
1419–HER SISTER'S CHILD

I would like to thank Lauren Newberg, the daughter of one of my dearest friends, for teaching me everything about horses, using her very own Spot and Ellie as patient models. I now know that horses can smile, because these two definitely do when Lauren's around.

And I'd like to thank friends Jerry and Linda Paradise for taking me on a special tour of their magnificent thoroughbred facility, Tuxedo Farms, in Ocala, Florida. Horses never had it so good.

CHAPTER ONE

BRADY WOUND through the crowd of Texas horsemen gathered in the show ring. The prime offering of the morning was coming into the arena next and everyone wanted a close-up view of Amber Mac.

Including Brady. He'd been excited about this young thoroughbred since Colin Warner had tipped him off to the horse's bloodlines and the private sale at Henley's Blue Bonnet Farm. Brady trusted Colin because Brady's good friend, Blake Smith, had hired the business whiz kid based on one interview. If Blake saw so much potential in Colin, that was all Brady needed to check out this horse for himself. And now, his future could very well hinge on whether or not he and his dad went home with Amber Mac.

He joined his father and the head trainer from Cross Fox Ranch in the center of the ring. Marshall Carrick rubbed his finger down his thick gray mustache. "Can you believe this crowd for mid-January?" he said. "I figured this being so soon after the holidays, everyone would be recovering from making merry. But apparently Al Henley got the word out that he was selling some prize stock before the spring auction."

"I hear ya', Dad. I just hope all these people haven't come to compete with us for Amber Mac."

Marshall cupped his hand over his mouth. "Blake and Warner seem to be right on about this animal and you can be sure Al knows what a winner he's got—he's invited enough people to ensure he'll rake in every dollar he can. I guess he spent too much on Christmas presents and needs to replenish his bank account with this sale." Keeping his voice low, Marshall turned to the man who'd been his head trainer for over thirty years. "Tell me one more time, Dobbs. The vet reports on Amber Mac are conclusive?"

Trevor Dobbs, stoop-shouldered from age but still clear-eyed and alert where horses were concerned, stared at his boss. "You know there's no such animal as the perfect horse, Marsh. But yes, the reports look good. The digital X-rays showed no imperfections. The horse's throat latch is wide-open. His lungs are clean."

Seeing someone he knew, Dobbs walked off. Marshall looked at Brady. "And the horse's conformation? You had another close look?"

"Of course, Dad. I told you before, I checked him over head to tail. His hocks and knees are straight. His neck is long. His eyes are wide and alert." Brady smiled. "In fact, I had a personal conversation with him and he seemed interested in everything I had to say."

Marshall tapped the sale catalog against his palm.

"You kid about this, but there's truth to what you just said. A horse that pays attention is easier to train."

"I know. You've told me. And this isn't my first day in the horse business. I grew up in it, remember?" He rubbed his knee. Standing for hours wasn't good for the old football injury. Stating a sad fact, he said, "Believe me, Dad, this horse is in better shape than I am."

"How about his hips?" Marshall asked.

"A bit narrow," Brady admitted. "But not enough to affect his running ability." He shook his head. "Look, you should examine him yourself. Then you wouldn't be questioning everything I'm telling you."

"I'll look at him when he comes out. I'm just making sure you haven't forgotten anything."

Brady tried to ignore his building resentment. "Either you trust me on this horse or you don't."

Marshall waved off his comment. "I trust you. But you haven't been home all that long."

"Almost a year and a half," Brady pointed out.

"I realize what this thoroughbred means to you. You've made it clear that you want me to consider you for Dobbs's position when he retires in six months. And since I won't do that just because you're my son—"

"I wouldn't expect you to. And I understand your reservations about me."

"—you need Amber Mac to prove you can take over from Dobbs. I get it, son… It's just that it's hard to keep up with the value of horseflesh while you're on a football field."

Or inside a casino. Brady knew the restraint his father must have used not to mention the sore subject of his son's ill-spent two years in Las Vegas. He wanted to point out that he'd been ready and willing to pull his weight in the family business since he'd come home. He kept silent, however, and watched as the gate at the end of the ring opened.

Henley's stable foreman coaxed Amber Mac into the ring. And every rancher from around the state paid attention.

"He's on a halter," Marshall said. "Is he bridle-broke?"

"Not yet," Brady said. He cast a sideways look at his father. "You can leave that up to me. Surely after thirty-two years of being a Carrick, I've proven to you that I can break horses to bridles and saddles." As the horse was led closer, Brady stared in awe. "Look at that deep chestnut color. And check his gait. A good swinging walk, long strides."

Al Henley came up behind them. "There he is, gentlemen. Amber Mac." He smiled with the slickness of a used-car salesman who knew he had serious customers on the lot. "In case I need to remind you, Mac's sire is Macintosh Red from Dufoil Stables in Virginia. Among his credits, Red won the Arkansas Derby, the Arlington Million and the Oak Leaf Stakes. His dam is our own Honey's Gold. She foaled Amber Mac in March."

"We know all that, Al," Marshall said. "It doesn't mean we're going to buy this horse."

Henley slapped Marshall on his back. "I think it does, Marsh. It's all about the bloodlines and you know this is a top-notch animal."

"I don't know anything of the sort," Marshall said. "He's carrying around that extra flesh we see in a lot of weanlings. What do you think, son?"

Brady hid a smile. "It's a shame, isn't it?" he said. "Means I'll have to put him on grass for a few weeks. Breeders should know better than to let a horse put on show fat."

Henley laughed. "Why don't you boys quit wasting time and make me an offer on this horse."

Marshall rubbed his chin. "I might take a chance on him. Like you said, his bloodlines are impressive. I'm prepared to offer you ten thousand."

Despite the cool January temperature, Brady removed his wide-brimmed hat and wiped the sweat from his brow. These two horse traders were a long way from coming to an agreement.

Henley scoffed at the offer. "Take Mac away," he instructed his stableman as he headed toward another group of potential buyers. "Find some serious horsemen in this crowd."

Brady started to protest, but Marshall lay a work-roughened hand on his shirtsleeve. "We can't appear too anxious, son. I wouldn't be surprised if Blue Bonnet had one of their own men in the crowd pretending to be interested in Mac." He smiled with one side of his mouth. "One thing you should remember about horse traders…you can't trust any of us. The best thing we can do now is have a look at that two-year-old Appaloosa over there and make Henley think we've lost interest."

At their truck forty-five minutes and several conversations later, Marshall Carrick took his checkbook from his glove compartment. "Not bad," he said as he wrote out the check. "I would have gone fifty grand on Mac, so I'm satisfied with forty-three thousand."

Dobbs passed around bottles of beer from a six-pack. "At least Henley's providing the refreshments."

Brady accepted the drink and took a long swallow. Forty-three thousand dollars. He knew his father had the money, but despite the fair salary Brady was earning at Cross Fox, it had been a long time since he'd seen five-digit figures in his own checking account. He figured it would take at least ten minutes for his heart to stop jumping into his throat.

"I'll find Al, pay our bill and make arrangements to pick up the horse," Marshall said, heading back to the show ring. He stopped and called over his shoulder. "I'm starved. Where'd you say that restaurant is you always go to, Dobbs?"

"Only a couple of miles down the road in Prairie Bend," the Irishman said. "Cliff's Diner. Best food in Texas."

"Meet you boys back here at the truck," Marshall said. "I'm hungry enough to eat a…" He stopped, chuckled. "Guess I won't say it."

Brady drained the rest of his beer. "I'll meet you

at the truck, too, Dobbs. I've got to have one more look at Amber Mac."

The trainer rested his arm on a fence post and smiled. "I thought you might."

CLIFF'S DINER was like a hundred others surviving in Texas prairie towns. It looked like an Airstream travel trailer on steroids, all silvery chrome on the outside and red, black and white on the inside. Brady waited for his father to slide into the vinyl booth then sat beside him. Dobbs settled across from them and opened one of the three menus the hostess had set on the table.

Marshall pushed his reading glasses to the end of his nose. "What's good?"

"The burgers," Dobbs said. "Half a pound each and brimming with juice 'long as you don't order them well done."

What the heck. Brady figured his arteries could stand a wake-up call. Besides, they were celebrating, and for a born-and-bred Texan, any celebration included beef. "So that's why you come here, to have a hamburger?"

"And the lemonade," Dobbs said. He leaned across the table. "Not to mention the best part..." A smile split the weathered creases of his face. "And there she is."

A cute, dark-haired waitress stopped at their table, an order pad open in her hand. "Hey, Dobbs," she said. "I haven't seen you around in a few months. No interesting horses over at the Blue Bonnet?"

"I don't come all the way up here from River Bluff

just to buy horses, darlin'. I come to see the prettiest waitress in Prairie Bend, maybe all of Texas. And if I'd known you were getting better looking every day, I'd have made the trip more often."

Brady stared at the trainer. Nearly all traces of Dobbs's Irish ancestry had vanished from his speech, though he still had the gift of the gab. The waitress was young enough to be his granddaughter. But Dobbs was about as faithful to his wife, Serafina, as any man could be.

The girl must have known it, as well, because she rolled her eyes. "Do you want lemonade with that blarney, Dobbs?"

He laughed. "Sure. But first I want you to meet my boss." He nodded toward Marshall. "This is the owner of Cross Fox Ranch, Marshall Carrick."

She stared at Marshall a moment before offering her hand across the table. "Nice to meet you."

"And this fella is his son, Brady," Dobbs said.

Brady glanced at the name tag on her red dress. "Hello, Molly."

She took a step back from the table. Her eyes widened as she appraised Brady overtly before grabbing her pen from her pocket and positioning it over the order pad. "Hi. So what'll you have?"

After taking down the orders, she headed toward the kitchen. Dobbs leaned back and smiled at Brady. "You've still got it, don't you?"

Brady stopped fiddling with a plastic carnation in the center of the table. "What are you talking about?"

"Didn't you see the way Molly looked at you? I can't tell you the last time a pretty young thing gave me the once-over. It's obvious Molly is a Cowboys fan."

Brady was used to curious, even adoring gazes from women. He hadn't had many in the past few years, but when he played with the Dallas Cowboys he'd gotten lots, even when he was married and had Daphne on his arm. But he'd swear the look he'd just gotten from Molly wasn't like that. In fact, she'd made him feel uncomfortable, as if she'd noticed he had something stuck between his teeth. He shook his head. "I didn't get the same impression, Dobbs."

"Then you weren't paying attention. I bet you've got a double-decker burger coming with the extra patty on the house." A busboy set three large glasses of lemonade on the table, and Dobbs took a swallow, while Marshall pulled out Amber Mac's sales receipt and ignored them. "Molly's cute, isn't she?" Dobbs said.

Looking over his shoulder, Brady watched her fill the coffee cup of a cowboy at the counter. She smiled at the guy, a warm natural expression unlike the reserved greeting she'd given Brady. She curled her fingers over her shapely hip and laughed, then excused herself with a flippant wave of her hand. Her wavy hair, bound in a ponytail, flirted with her nape as she walked away. "Yeah, she's cute," Brady agreed. "How long have you known her?"

"A while," Dobbs said. "She was working at this diner when I started coming here almost ten years ago. Back then I seem to remember she was married. Then she was gone for a few years. And one day she was back and no ring on her finger."

Dobbs looked at the artificial plants hanging from the ceiling. A pitiful strand of tinsel drooped from one of them, overlooked when the Christmas decorations had been packed up. "I asked her why she hadn't hooked up with someone again," he added.

Oddly curious about the answer, Brady said, "What'd she say?"

"She's a wisecracker. She went on about how any girl would be happy to have a permanent spot at Cliff's Diner and that she'd probably be serving up lemonade when her hair turned gray." He shook his head. "I hope that's not true."

"Hush now," Marshall said, looking up. "Here she comes with our food."

Molly set plates in front of the men, asked if they needed anything else and walked away.

"Eat up," Marshall said. "We've got a horse to take home this afternoon."

As they ate, each man expounded on the virtues of Amber Mac and the possibility of the thoroughbred becoming the newest horse-racing sensation.

Brady washed down a bite of hamburger with some lemonade. No time like the present to state his case. "Let me train him, Dad."

Marshall put his burger down. "Whoa, son. That's a powerful ambition from a guy who, until just recently, had no interest in the business."

"I never said that. Anyway, I've been involved since I returned from Vegas—"

"As a front-office man," Marshall said. "You have a lot to learn about training a racehorse."

Brady frowned. "Right. And I won't get much experience as long as you use me to meet with track execs and state gaming officials."

"You'll get your chance," Marshall said. "A face man is what we need now. You've done a lot for the Cross Fox image since you've been back. People like you. They're impressed by you."

"They're impressed by my football stats, you mean."

Marshall didn't argue.

"Look, Dad, I can train Amber Mac. What I haven't learned from you all these years, Dobbs taught me. I'm ready. It's what I want to do. If I'm going to build a reputation as a trainer and restore your confidence in me, I'd like to start with this colt."

Marshall stared at him. "I'm sure you would. But I don't know if I'm ready to put the future of a forty-three-thousand-dollar thoroughbred on a rookie trainer, even if he is my son." Marshall was never one to pull any punches. "Besides, how do I know you won't get another burr under your saddle and take off? How do I know you won't end up in Vegas at the end of a craps table again?"

Brady bit back a retort. How many times did he have to hear this? Marshall had been in favor of his son's decision to play with the Cowboys after college. But when Brady's knee injury ended his career—and his marriage—Marshall certainly hadn't approved of Brady's decision to try his luck as a professional player in Las Vegas.

"Look, Dad," he said through clenched teeth. "Forget about the past. It's over and I'm here to stay."

"And I'm glad of it," Marshall said. "Cross Fox is your home. And as long as you only scratch your gambling itch with your local poker games, I've got no complaints. A man's got to have a few vices."

"Well, you're welcome to scratch your own itch this week," Brady muttered, glad to change the topic. "The game's tonight and I told Jake I'd be back in time to make it. There'll probably be some open chairs. Do either of you want to come?"

Marshall frowned. "Jake? That means he's hosting in the old Wild Card Saloon."

"Yeah."

"Count me out. That place is still a wreck. Sat empty for too long and Jake's uncle sure never took care of it."

"Jake's taking interest in it now that he decided not to sell," Brady explained. "He and Cole are fixing it up. It's looking pretty good."

"I'll believe it when I see it," Marshall said. "Look, I like Jake Chandler. But you'd better not mention to your mother that you're hanging out with him again. She still thinks he was a bad influence on you."

"That's ridiculous." Brady slammed his lemonade down harder than he'd intended. "If anything, back when we were in high school, it was the other way around. Or at least it was mutual. Why do you think everyone called us the Wild Bunch?"

Marshall put his hands up in a gesture of defeat. "Hey, I'm willing to give Jake a chance. I'm just warning you that your mother hasn't forgiven or forgotten his antics in high school."

Brady turned to Dobbs. "What about you? Want to play?"

"I'll be bushed after riding in the truck with you guys for four hours," Dobbs said.

"Suit yourselves." When he returned home from Vegas, Brady realized how much he'd missed his friends from River Bluff, men in their thirties now with adult problems and ambitions. Some of them had strayed, as Brady had, to different parts of the world, but now they were back and playing a weekly Texas Hold 'Em poker game. And for Brady, at this time in his life, the friendly wagering and camaraderie were just what he needed.

Dobbs popped the last of his burger into his mouth and followed it with a ketchup-soaked fry. "Still, if you ask me, it's a damn shame."

Brady gave him a quizzical look. "What is?"

"You're the best poker player I know. You've got good instincts and all those college smarts. I just think if you'd stuck with poker up there in Vegas, you would have won a big tournament and been set for life."

Brady held up his hand hoping to erase the scowl on his father's face. "I left when I should have—I was losing more than just money."

Dobbs pushed his plate away and brushed a shock of graying red hair off his forehead. "You coulda' won though, couldn't you?" he coaxed. "It's just the three of us now, Brady. You can level with us. You were good enough for the big tournaments. You coulda' won some big pots."

Brady rubbed his hand down his face. He smiled at Dobbs. "Yeah, I could have won. But before you start thinking I'm some sort of poker god, let me tell you something. Anybody can win at the big tournaments—and anybody can lose. With intensive study of poker odds, some training in reading opponents and money management and the proper alignment of the planets, almost anybody can be coached to win."

Dobbs leaned forward. "You really think so?"

"Sure. Poker's more skill than luck."

"So if you wanted to, you could take some cowpoke off the street and teach him the game?"

Brady considered his answer for a moment. "Cowpoke, politician, garbage collector. Anybody with an average level of intelligence can be taught. And yes, I could teach him."

Marshall chuckled. "I see you haven't lost that old Carrick confidence, son."

His dad was wrong. A career-ending knee injury, a failed marriage and a foolish run at the most player-unfriendly games in Vegas had destroyed his confidence. Not to mention the life-altering tragedy that forced Brady to pack up and leave on the next plane for San Antonio. But he was trying to get his self-respect back. He was finding some of it at the weekly poker game where he generally won more than his share of pots.

"I'd be happy to prove it to you," he said. "You pick the person, Dad, and I'll teach him to play. The quarter finals of the U.S. Poker Play-offs is coming up in just a little more than five weeks. I'll bet you I can coach that guy into a seat at the final table."

Marshall covered his shock with a belly laugh. "Interesting bet. Just exactly what are we wagering on, Brady?"

This conversation had suddenly taken a serious turn. For a second Brady wondered if he was getting in over his head. But he quickly banished that thought. He was a damn good poker player. "Tell you what, Dad. If I have your pick at the final table in the USP, you give me training rights to Amber Mac."

Marshall sobered. "Big talk, Brady."

"You think I can't do it?"

"That's right," he said. "I think you can't do it."

Brady wasn't about to back down. He knew his dad well enough to know that the gambler in him was intrigued. "Then what have you got to lose? Try me."

Marshall looked at Dobbs. "What do you think? Should we give this upstart a chance to eat his words?"

"I don't know." Dobbs considered. "What do we get out of it if the kid loses the bet?"

Brady smiled. "I'll pay your entry fees at the local game for one year."

Both men eyed each other over the table. Hundreds of dollars were now at stake, making this a serious bet. "And we get to pick the person for the wager?" Marshall asked.

"You pick. But be reasonable. The guy has to be of age and have moderate intelligence."

At that moment, Molly cleared her throat and tapped on her order pad. "Sorry to interrupt such momentous wagering, boys, but I thought you might want to bet on who gets the check."

Dobbs chuckled before sitting back and leveling a serious look at her. "What about Molly?" he said to Marshall. "She's clever."

Brady glanced at Dobbs. He couldn't be serious.

"Now, hold on, gentlemen," she said. "My name has just been mentioned in the same conversation with the word *wager*. That's enough to make anybody nervous."

"Don't be," Dobbs said. "I'm presenting you with the chance of a lifetime. How would you like to be a student of Brady's for a five-week course?"

She frowned. Not exactly a reaction designed to boost a guy's ego, Brady thought, even if they were just kidding around.

"I don't know anything about racehorses," she said.

Dobbs grinned. "We're not talking about horses. We're talking about poker."

"I know even less about that."

Dobbs looked at the other two. "See? She's perfect."

Molly took a step back. "Perfect for what?"

Dobbs gave her a grin that was part confident

Texan and part cocky Irishman. "What do you say, sweetheart? You want to come to River Bluff and learn to play poker from a master?"

CHAPTER TWO

POKER? Molly couldn't suppress an unladylike bark of laughter. Her father would heat under the collar of his clerical robe if he knew she was about to even participate in a conversation about gambling. There wasn't even a deck of cards in the modest house she shared with Luther Whelan.

She stared at Marshall Carrick, the man who carried the weight of Cross Fox Ranch on his broad shoulders, and waited for him to say something to make sense of this. When he didn't, she picked up one of the empty glasses on the table and made a show of sniffing it. "I'm thinking you boys have been sipping something a whole lot stronger than lemonade."

Brady smiled, an easy full-bodied grin that had her believing he could talk people into almost anything, just as she knew he had. The younger Carrick resembled his father in stature and size. But Brady's bronzed complexion was less weathered. His light brown hair was sun-streaked and just long enough to fall over his forehead. The collar of his blue oxford-cloth shirt had a distinctive lack of

Western ornamentation. Unusual for a horseman in the heart of Texas.

"It's okay, Molly," Brady said, his voice a smooth, cultured version of typical ranch-hand drawl. "We were just playing a game of 'what if' over lunch."

Dobbs leaned forward. "'What if?' So now you're backing out?"

"No. But there isn't any reason to get Molly mixed up in this."

"Of course there is," Dobbs insisted. "We picked her."

"This is getting weird." Molly waved the check in the air. "Who's going to pay this bill?"

Dobbs pointed to Brady. "Mr. Big Shot."

Brady pulled his wallet out of his jeans.

"Here's the thing, Molly," Dobbs said. "Brady claims he can take a novice card player and lead him—or her—all the way to a final table at the Texas Hold 'Em quarter finals U.S. Poker Play-offs in Las Vegas in February."

Molly had some knowledge of Texas Hold 'Em. Her husband, Kevin, had played the game when he was away on the rodeo circuit. "I've seen that on TV."

"Sure you have," Dobbs said. "The players that get to the last table in just the quarter finals can win, what, Brady? Thousands of dollars?"

He nodded. "This quarterly event draws mostly local players, and even sixth place can be a decent payoff."

She pointed her pen at him. "And you think you

can coach somebody who's never played before to the final table?"

He shrugged. "Look, we were just shooting off steam."

Marshall leaned back and smiled. "So you're saying you can't do it now?"

Brady scowled. "I can do it. But Molly doesn't want to be involved. She must be thinking we're crazy."

"She's involved already," Dobbs said. "I told you—we picked her, didn't we Marshall?"

"We were sure talking about it."

"And Brady said it was our choice."

"Yep, he did."

Brady folded some bills in his hand. "Don't let us keep you, Molly. Do I pay you or up at the counter?"

Determined he wasn't about to put her off, she stared into the deepest green eyes she'd ever seen. "Pay me. And you're not keeping me. It's almost time for my break. I've known Dobbs for years. If he says they picked me for this wager, then I guess that puts the cards on my table."

Brady chuckled, but it seemed a self-conscious effort to appear unruffled. He handed her the money.

She tucked it into her pocket. "So you can do it? You can teach me to play poker?"

"Sure, I could, but..."

"What would you get out of this?" she asked. "What's at stake for you?"

"It's personal."

"Tell her," Marshall said. "She's got a right to

know what we're betting on."

Brady stared at his father a good long moment before he said, "Not that I think that's true, but okay." He looked up at her. "I win the right to train the horse we just bought."

"And this is important to you?" Molly said.

He didn't answer that. He didn't have to. The fire in his eyes was proof enough. "I see that it is," she added.

Brady darted a quick uncomfortable glance at his companions before turning back to Molly. "But look, all that doesn't matter. You have to understand what it would take to get to the final table. Long hours. Personal sacrifice. This is a tough training regimen for a woman."

"For a *woman?*" Molly repeated.

Brady looked down. "Don't take that the wrong way."

The part of Molly that her father said she inherited from her mother and called her "rebel soul" flared to life. She was suddenly interested in this proposition for two reasons. She stated the first one. "If I won, would I get to keep the money?"

Marshall muffled his laughter behind his cupped hand. Dobbs didn't even try.

"I don't know," Brady said. "We'd have to work that out. But we could come up with a fair split I suppose." He shook his head, glared at Dobbs. "Look, I'm sorry we brought this up. Like I said, it's a crazy idea and you can't seriously be thinking of pursuing it."

Oh, but she was. After all these years of Trevor

Dobbs coming into this diner, fate had finally sent the legend of Cross Fox Ranch himself, Brady Carrick. Who was Molly Davis to spit in the eye of fate?

The name Brady Carrick had been playing like a sad movie in her head for a year and a half now. Every time she cried herself to sleep. Every time she carried another plate of runny eggs to a table in the diner. Every time she tried to tell her son why his daddy wasn't coming home. So even without the substantial financial payoff he'd mentioned, reason number two for considering this would be incentive enough. She could ease some of that heartache Brady Carrick had inflicted on her and let him finance her way to a new beginning.

She'd never get her life back the way it was, but just maybe the guy who stood to inherit Cross Fox Ranch would pay for what he'd done to Kevin by helping his widow and son start over. If she won, she could buy a nice, cozy house for her and Sam far away from Prairie Bend and the rules set by Luther Whelan. She stacked the empty plates from the table and gave the men her most winning smile. No matter what happened, she had to think of the tip.

Brady slid out of his seat. "It was nice meeting you, Molly."

The first signs of panic tingled down her spine. They were leaving. "Have a good trip back," she said.

The three walked out of the restaurant, and Molly went over to the cash register. Struggling with a mountain of indecision, she absently passed the money over the counter. *You'd better do something pretty darn quick, Molly Jean,* she said to herself. *When these men drive out of the parking lot, they're taking your opportunity with them. You'll probably never see Brady Carrick again or get the chance to make him pay.*

She watched out the window as the men crossed the lot to a pickup truck with a horse trailer hitched to the back. Brady opened the driver's side door and got in, and in that split second she made up her mind.

"I'm going on break, Uncle Cliff."

He picked up the money. "Okay, but hurry back. I need you to fill the ketchup bottles."

She headed to the door.

"Wait a minute, Molly," her uncle called. "Your tip's in here."

She hurried back. The lunch tab had been just under twenty-two dollars, and Brady had given her thirty. She took the eight dollars change and stuffed it in her pocket.

"That's a good tip," Cliff said.

"Yeah." Though she definitely needed the money, she grumbled to herself, "No wonder Dobbs called him Mr. Big Shot."

LEANING OVER to look out the passenger door, Brady watched Molly come across the parking lot. A cool breeze whipped the ends of her ponytail around her face and shaped her skirt to the curvy outline of her legs. Brady couldn't look away. For a moment he imagined her in the hill country around River Bluff standing on a rolling green crest, not here in a dusty diner parking lot.

"Look there," Dobbs said. "Molly's walking over."

Brady patted his pockets. "We must have left something on the table. Did either of you forget something?"

Marshall shook his head. "Got my wallet and checkbook. Cell phone's in the glove box."

Brady set his elbow on the steering wheel. "Then what does she want?"

"Only one way to find out," Dobbs said. "Hush up and listen."

She stopped within a few feet of the open door, where Marshall and Dobbs stood. She leaned over to peer into the truck cab at Brady. "Something wrong?" he said.

"No. Just came out here to tell you I'll do it."

He knew darned well what she meant, but he needed to buy time to catch his breath. "Do what?"

"I'll learn poker."

Dobbs slapped his thigh. "Hot damn. That's what I like. A woman with gumption."

Brady gave him a warning glare, got out of the truck and walked around to her. "You can't be serious."

"You keep saying that. But I am."

"Look, we were just kidding in there."

"I wasn't," Dobbs said. "You weren't serious about wanting to train Amber Mac?"

Brady narrowed his eyes. "You know I meant every word of that."

"Then I can only assume you meant every word of the wager."

Marshall smiled in a noncommittal sort of way. "I heard the bet. It was clear to me. But I'm going to leave this up to the three of you."

Brady stared at Molly. She held his gaze with about as much determination as he'd ever seen. "I can't let you do this," he said. "First of all, I've never played poker with a…"

Her eyes sparked, just enough for him to know that what he was about to say had better stop before it left his mouth. Hell, he loved women, considered them different but equal, and he was comfortable with that view of the sexes. Especially the different part. But he didn't know if he could enjoy his appreciation for feminine virtues over the green felt of a poker table.

She arched her eyebrows, took a step forward. "You don't have a problem teaching poker to a woman, do you?"

He held up his hand and hoped she believed him when he said, "Of course not. But you've got to give this a lot of thought."

"I have. And I'm not agreeing to this lightly. I've watched poker tournaments on TV. The game doesn't look all that hard to me. I can learn it and I can sure use the money."

It was as if a whole bale had just dropped down in front of him and he had to start grasping for every straw he could get his hands on. "But what about your job? You'd have to leave it to come to Cross Fox in River Bluff."

She feigned a sorrowful look over her shoulder. "Leaving all this would be a real shame, wouldn't it?"

"And what about family? There must be people who would worry about you."

"I wouldn't be leaving anybody that matters." She pointed through the window. "See that man at the counter?"

Brady looked at the middle-aged guy behind the cash register. "Yeah."

"That's Cliff. He owns the diner and he's my uncle. As long as there's a waitress here to fill the ketchup bottles, he won't miss me."

Brady figured there had to be someone in her life who could raise hell if she took off, so he asked the most important question. "Are you married?"

"No."

He thought of the cowboy she'd flirted with a while ago. "Have you got a brawny boyfriend with a high-voltage ego who'd come after you?"

"No."

"How about other responsibilities? You must have bills here, maybe a mortgage."

"No. Free and clear."

There was something about her. Her determination impressed him even as it warned him about possible complications down the road. "How will you get by financially if you leave your job?"

"That needs to be a condition of my training. It's five weeks?"

"About that."

"You'll have to pay my board. It's only fair." She didn't even blink.

Brady raked his hand through his hair. He was beginning to wonder just what this woman might consider "only fair" once the training had begun. But then he pictured Amber Mac, the finest horse he'd ever laid eyes on. Maybe the bet was crazy, but the consequences were real enough. His father was a man of his word and if he said Brady could train the horse if he won this bet, then that's what would happen.

He gave Molly a serious head-to-toe appraisal. She stared right back at him. She had guts. Her answers were quick and decisive. She was obviously ambitious and she wasn't afraid of taking a risk. These were all good qualities in a poker player. Maybe this would work out. All he had to do was set some limits, let her know he was the boss. If she listened and worked hard, he could make her a success at the U.S. Poker Play-offs. After all, the world of high-stakes poker was full of exciting underdog stories and Molly from Cliff's Diner might be another one.

She placed her hands on her hips. "I don't know what you're thinking about, Brady, but I've got to have an answer. My break's over and there are some hungry cowboys inside who want their lunch." Never flinching, she added, "I can do this. You won't be sorry. So what'll it be?"

He pulled out a business card for Cross Fox Ranch and handed it to her. "You think about this very carefully. If it doesn't work and you don't end up with a nice bankroll, you might want to make sure your uncle will give you your job back. At the end of five weeks, win or lose, it's over. You've got to understand that."

She put the card in her pocket. "No problem."

He got his hat from the cab, smoothed his hair back and pulled the crown of the felt Wrangler low over his brow. "We've got to go. If I see you, I see you. But don't wait too long. If I don't do this with you, I'll be looking for someone else."

"Fair enough."

He turned to head back around the truck but stopped and allowed himself one more lingering look at her. "You know where I am?"

"I do."

Brady was damn sure it would be the last time he ever saw Molly and, surprisingly, he was feeling bad about that. He got in the truck. Marshall climbed in beside him followed by Dobbs, who gave Molly a thumbs-up. As he pulled out of the parking lot, Brady looked in the side-view mirror. The tires had kicked up a good bit of dust, but he could see her walking back toward the diner, a sway in her hips. "I expect that's the end of the wager," he said to the other guys.

"You're probably right," Marshall said. "And it's for the best I suppose. But it was a fun diversion while it lasted."

Dobbs smiled. "You boys don't know Molly."

Clifford Whelan set his spatula next to the hot grill and wiped his hands on his apron. He didn't like filling in for the diner's short-order cook, but Jessie had gotten off early to take his daughter to the doctor. Already grumpy, Cliff scowled at his niece. "What do you mean you won't be in to work tomorrow?"

"You weren't listening, Uncle Cliff," she said. "I told you I might not be in at all after today."

"What are you talking about?"

She pinned a lunch order to the wheel under the warming lights. "I'm taking a long vacation, maybe a permanent one."

"You can't do that. I need you here. You've got to give notice."

"You'll be fine," she said. "Madge's sister, Junie, wants a job. I'll tell Madge to have her show up in the morning. June's a real nice girl, a quick learner."

Cliff frowned, picked up the spatula and flipped a row of burgers. "What kind of vacation are you talking about? I've never known you to just take off. Where are you going?"

She sighed. He was right. Molly couldn't remember ever having a true vacation in all her thirty years. As a child, she'd gone with her father to religious conferences, not much fun for a girl who found rules hard to follow. Her so-called vacations didn't get much better when she was married to Kevin. Before Sam was born, she'd traipse along with her husband to dusty show arenas and the low-budget motels that catered to rodeo cowboys. Since this trip wasn't for pleasure, either, she'd definitely given her uncle a false impression of her plans.

"I'm going south, around San Antonio," she told him.

Cliff layered cheese on all the burgers. "Who do you know in San Antone?"

"I've got friends there."

He gave her a suspicious glance. "Since when?"

Since a half hour ago, and I can't really say they're friends. "Since I went to community college," she lied. "They've invited me and Sam to come stay a while. I might even get a job there."

"What does your daddy have to say about this?"

"He doesn't exactly know yet."

Cliff blew out a long breath. "Oh, great. I don't want to be around when he hears this."

Molly coughed.

"He does care about you, Molly." Cliff smiled. "And he's awfully fond of Sam. Talks about him all the time. And remember, he took you in when Kevin died."

"Of course I remember that—I've thanked him at least a hundred times." *Despite having to listen to him rant about what a terrible husband Kevin was.*

"Plus, he's gotten used to having you run his house."

She reached for a pair of platters her uncle had set under the lights. "Right. He's fine with me cooking and cleaning, so long as I don't complain about the rules or interrupt him when he's telling me what a mess I've made of my life."

Cliff conceded her analysis with a nod. "He's a hard man to live with. He never got over your mother running out."

Molly pushed that bad memory to the back of her

mind. Her father wasn't the only one who'd suffered over her mother's abandonment. She checked the orders to make sure they were correct. "He'll just have to get by without me," she said. "This is an opportunity for us and I'd be stupid to pass it up."

"What are you going to do about Sam's school?"

"He'll only miss tomorrow and Friday. And it's only second grade. I'll get him into a class on Monday in the new place."

He gave her a fatherly look. "You got money enough to move on? I might be able to lend you a few bucks."

She smiled at him. Cliff really was a kind man, nothing like his brother. While Cliff, with a couple dozen excess pounds, was a soft and comfy-looking man, Luther Whelan was all sharp bones and unforgiving angles. Molly often wished she'd been born to Cliff instead of Luther. Then, as a young girl she would have had a lap to sit on, and maybe her mother would have stuck around. "We'll be fine," she said, hating the hint of doubt in her voice. "I've got some savings."

She headed toward the dining area with the plates. "Don't tell Dad about this before I've had a chance," she called over her shoulder. "I think he should hear it from me first."

Cliff snickered. "You don't have to worry about that. I'm not going near your house tonight." He read the next order on the wheel and got back to work. "One more thing, Molly…"

She turned around. "What?"

"You take care of yourself. Life hasn't been easy for you the last year or so. If this adventure of yours doesn't work out the way you planned, you come on home. There will always be a place for you here at the diner."

"Thanks, Uncle Cliff. That means a lot to me."

MOLLY STOPPED at a drugstore on her way to pick Sam up at school and bought a map of Texas. Next she stopped at the bank and withdrew her entire savings, two thousand three hundred and twelve dollars. Not a fortune, but enough to get by for a couple of weeks if things didn't work out at Cross Fox Ranch. And she had her credit card, which, thankfully, now had a low balance. At least she'd accomplished something worthwhile since Kevin had died. Living with her father, she'd managed to pay off some bills she and her husband had accumulated.

By the time she pulled into the driveway at her father's house, Molly had a plan. When she reached River Bluff, her first stop would be Cross Fox Ranch. She'd told Brady Carrick he'd be responsible for her board, but even if that didn't work out, she and Sam could stay in a motel while she looked for a part-time job. While Sam was at school, she'd divide her time between job hunting and learning poker.

If she eventually won a big pot in Vegas, then her future would be secure. She'd put that money toward opening a consignment shop for kids' clothes. She'd got the idea when she was pregnant with Sam and picking up second-hand baby clothes and supplies. Maybe she'd even open up shop in

River Bluff if she liked the small town. With her two years of college math, she could run a bookkeeping service on the side.

And if I don't win at the U.S. Poker Play-offs... Molly unlocked the front door of her father's house, followed Sam inside and set her purse on the hall table. *Well, Uncle Cliff said there was always a place for me at the diner. It's not like I haven't gone back before.*

She smiled at Sam. "You want some cookies, cowboy?"

He nodded, and went to the sink to wash his hands before sitting at the kitchen table. She set him up with milk and Oreos, sat beside him and ran her fingers through his sandy-brown hair. "Where's that happy face, Sammy?"

His lips curled up at the edges in an effort to please her, and Molly's heart ached. Sam didn't smile nearly enough for a seven-year-old. Maybe all that would change once they got away from this stifling environment.

She glanced at the kitchen clock. Three-thirty. Her father would be home soon. He would meditate for an hour and then expect dinner promptly at six. She could depend on that. Luther Whelan never altered his schedule.

AT SEVEN-THIRTY, after she'd put the last dinner plate in the cupboard, Molly checked to make sure Sam's door was closed and then went into the living room to face her father. Engrossed in the newspaper, he didn't acknowledge her when she came in the room. "Dad?"

He looked up. "What is it?"

"I need to talk to you."

He set his spectacles on the end table. "What's wrong now?"

"Nothing's wrong," she said. "I just have news."

He waited.

"I'm leaving Prairie Bend tomorrow. Sam and I are moving."

He set the newspaper on his lap. "Don't talk nonsense, Molly Jean."

"It's not nonsense." She used the same lie she'd told Uncle Cliff earlier. "Friends have asked me to come to the San Antonio area. I have a job lined up that will support Sam and me..."

He looked around his neat, uncomplicated living room. "You don't need to go anywhere. You've got everything a woman could want right here. I take care of you better than that husband of yours ever did."

"I know you provide a home for us, Dad, but it's not enough. Not for me and not for Sam."

He glowered at her. "You're not taking my grandson away," he stated as if it were an indisputable fact.

"Sam is my son. He's going where I go."

"I won't hear of it. Sam needs a strong hand, which he won't get under your influence. If that mistake of a marriage didn't teach you that—"

"A discussion of my marriage and my son is off-limits." Molly's stomach churned.

He exhaled deeply. "Have you forgotten that I took you back in after that…that rodeo bum died?"

"No, and I'm grateful, but that's in the past. You don't have to bring it up again."

"Fine. Then let's talk about how this irrational decision will affect me." He rolled the newspaper and pointed it at her. "Have you considered how your actions will embarrass me in front of my congregation again? I've raised you on my own, Molly. It wasn't easy after your mother left, but I've tried to teach you proper values. And all I've received for my effort is disrespect. I won't let you make a mockery of my position in this community again."

He wouldn't even hear her out. He didn't care about her feelings, her needs, just like he probably never cared about her mother's. Molly stared at the floor, anywhere but at the fire of self-righteousness in her father's eyes. For a man who professed to dedicate his life to forgiveness and tolerance, Luther Whelan had a hard time showing either of those to his own daughter.

But then, Molly had known how he would react. She'd made sure Sam was busy with his toys in his room so he wouldn't have to listen to his grandfather's harsh words, but it was a small house and she was afraid he was hearing everything. Maybe her father did care about her in his own emotionally bereft way, but the environment he provided was void of real human interaction and she had to get out. She wasn't about to back down.

The newspaper rattled in his hands and Molly looked up. "I won't take you back," he said. "If you go, it's forever."

"I don't want to leave like this, Dad," she said. "But I'm going. I'm sorry—"

"You're never sorry," he snapped. "Those are empty words from a woman who doesn't think of anyone but herself." And then he said the words designed to hurt her the most. "You're just like your mother."

"Leave her be, Luther."

Cliff walked into the room from the kitchen, silencing both of them. "It's her life. She's going and that's that."

Molly nearly cried. Despite his promise not to come to the house tonight, he was here. She could have kissed him right there on the spot.

"This isn't your concern, Cliff," Luther said.

"I'm making it my concern. Molly's a good girl. She deserves a chance to get out of this place."

"I won't take her in when she comes crawling back."

"You won't have to. If she needs to, she can stay with Edith and me."

Uncle Cliff waved her out of the room, asking her if she didn't have suitcases she needed to pack. Grateful, Molly escaped any further recrimination from her father.

Now Uncle Cliff was gone and her dad sat on the front porch in the chilly January air, no doubt trying to figure out how his only child could have strayed so far. And he didn't even know that her plans involved gambling.

At nine o'clock Molly stretched out on the twin bed next to her son, propped a pillow behind her back and crossed her ankles. She twisted the cowboy lamp on the nightstand so its light fell on the map in her lap. "You want to see where we're going tomorrow?" she asked Sam.

"Sure, Mama. Is it a long way?"

"It's pretty far. We're starting here on this big road called Highway 35..." she traced a line south with her finger "...all the way to another highway, which leads us to River Bluff. That's where we'll stop."

"How long will it take us to get there?"

"I'd say about four hours, depending on how often we stop." She smiled at him. "Part of the fun of traveling is stopping along the road."

Sam looked up at her, a worried frown marring his chubby angelic features. "I don't think it'll be fun at all."

"For heaven's sake, why not?"

"'Cause when Grandpa found out we were going, he was plenty mad. So it must not be a fun thing to do."

"You shouldn't worry about Grandpa, baby," she said. "He won't stay mad. Why, I'll bet that in a day or two he'll have forgotten he was angry and will want to hear all about our adventure!" If there was a way to keep communications open between her father and her son, Molly would. "You can write him a letter if you want. He'd like that."

Molly wrapped her arm around Sam's shoulders

and pulled him close. "Besides, I think we're going to have lots of fun. And if we don't, then we'll go someplace else. Texas is a big state." She held up the map to illustrate her point. "Maybe you can pick the place next time." She stood up, kissed his cheek and turned off the lamp. "Just go to sleep now, Sammy. I'm going to stay in your room a while to pack up your things."

She handed him his favorite stuffed pony and he snuggled into his blankets. "G'night, Mama."

By the faint glow of his nightlight, she neatly folded his clothes into a suitcase. While she worked, the last moments between her father and her uncle played in her mind. Luther had said he was sick and tired of dealing with the mistakes his daughter made of her life and trying to explain to his congregation how a supposedly God-fearing child could grow up to cast such a shadow of shame over her family name.

Sometime, years ago, her father had stopped thinking of Molly as an individual and began to see her as an extension of her mother. Two women whose identical sinful natures conspired to ruin his life and reputation. That was sad, but Molly couldn't do anything about it. Maybe she *was* too much like her mother. And maybe she wanted to be.

She closed Sam's suitcase and filled a box with his favorite toys. Thinking he was asleep, she tiptoed to the door. "Mama?"

She looked back at the bed. Sam lay perfectly still, but his voice was hoarse with a little boy's determination. "I think I'll wait and see if Grandpa writes me first."

"That's fine, sweetie."

She left the room more convinced than ever that she and her son were two people very much in need of an adventure.

CHAPTER THREE

BRADY HUNG HIS HAT on a hook in the mudroom and left his boots by the back door. After washing his hands at the utility tub, he went to the kitchen where he snuck up behind Ruby, the woman who'd been the family cook since he was a boy, and kissed her warm brown neck. She swatted at him. "I knew you were back there," she said. "You can't surprise me anymore. Not since you've grown four feet and put on a hundred pounds."

He laughed. "I guess a six-foot-three man has lost some of the upper hand when it comes to surprise attacks."

She tried not to smile. "You wash those hands?"

"Yes, ma'am."

"You hungry?"

"You need to ask?"

"Go on in the sunroom. Your daddy wanted lunch in there today. I've got it set up on the buffet."

He went down the hallway past his father's study, a guest bathroom and the formal dining room and entered the cheerful six-sided glassed-in area his mother had designed when the house was built. She referred to it as the conservatory and filled it with hanging ferns and philodendron, but everyone else called it the sunroom.

Marshall set down his newspaper and looked closely at Brady. "Late night?" he said.

"You could say that."

"Did you win at least?"

"Came out okay despite having a lot on my mind." He glanced at his father's plate and the remains of something once smothered in gravy. Another test for Brady's arteries, but whatever was in the chafing dish smelled too good to pass up. He headed to the buffet table. "I'm guessing stew," he said.

"Ruby's specialty. And mighty tasty."

Brady ladled two helpings onto a plate, picked up a couple of biscuits from under a cloth napkin and chose a seat across the table from his father. "Where's Mom?"

"Still sleeping, I guess," Marshall said. "I was beat when we got home from Henley's last night and turned in early. Angela was still in the den. I don't know what time she came upstairs."

Brady was sorry to hear this news. Before he'd left for the poker game, he'd come to the house to tell his mother about Amber Mac. It was after dark and he'd found her in front of the television. She was staring vacantly at an old black-and-white movie and he saw a drink in her hand. It only took a minute for him to realize she'd obviously started drinking at the cocktail hour and had continued with rum and Cokes well into the evening. Her interest in the new colt had been cool at best.

"Are you still having the hoedown on Sunday?" The annual event, which began at Cross Fox twenty-nine years ago to celebrate Marshall's thirtieth birthday had become a Carrick family tradition. Brady figured his dad might cancel the party if Angela wasn't up to hosting.

Marshall furrowed his brow. "Of course. Folks expect it. Besides, a man can't stop living just because…" He never finished his thought and instead went to the buffet, filled a bowl with peaches and poured heavy cream over the top. "Are any of your friends from the poker game coming?"

Brady had invited Blake, Cole, Jake and Luke, the four regulars on Texas Hold 'Em nights. "Yes, they're coming. Along with their girlfriends and wives." Marshall knew Blake's wife, Annie. She was a reporter for the River Bluff newspaper and expecting their first child. And Brady figured his dad would remember Rachel Diamonte, a former River Bluff prom queen, who'd recently come back to town. She and Jake had a history to mend, but since he'd hired her to renovate the bar they'd worked out their differences and were planning a future together. But he'd never met Tessa, the new love of Cole Lawry's life.

"So Jake's coming to the party?" Marshall said.

"Yep. Mom's just going to have to accept that."

"It'll be all right. Your mother likes Luke, at least. There's no better people than that whole Chisum clan."

They ate in silence until Marshall scooped the last of the fruit from his bowl. He sat back. "Did you time those three-year-olds on the half mile this morning?"

"Sure did. Jodie's Girl cut five seconds off her previous time. I breezed the two stallions with her, but they didn't improve. In my opinion, though, Jodie's ready for a claiming race."

Marshall nodded. "She's a good strong filly. How's Amber Mac today?"

"Seems okay. I'm going to feed him when I'm done here."

"Not too much. He's not showing hog fat, but we've got to trim him down anyway."

"I know, Dad. We talked about this. I won't overfeed him." Brady sopped up a pool of gravy with a biscuit. "At breakfast I went over the vet reports on him again. His vaccinations are up-to-date and his vitamin regimen seems appropriate for his age and weight." He pushed his plate back and stood. He shouldn't have to prove himself to his father every time they talked, yet he constantly felt the need to. "I've got to go, Dad. See you later."

Marshall picked up his paper and resumed reading.

Brady returned to the mudroom for his boots and hat. He left by the back entrance and headed across the two hundred yards of lush green lawn that separated the stables from the house. He regretted not taking the golf cart…his knee was acting up. But he believed in the old-fashioned theory that pain can be walked off. Dodger, the family's Jack Russell terrier yapped at his heels. "Where did you come from? I didn't see you begging for scraps at lunch."

The dog alternated between scuttling on his belly and nipping at the hem of Brady's jeans. "Calm down. And stop that barking. We're almost at the stables. You're supposed to be a horse's companion, not his biggest aggravation."

They reached the stalls and Brady told Dodger to stay put, out of sight of Amber Mac. Predictably, the terrier didn't pay any mind. Instead, he scratched at the bottom half of Mac's door and resumed yipping. Amber Mac reared, hitting his rump against the back of the stall.

At the sound of laughter behind him, Brady whirled around. Dobbs picked up Dodger, set him in the yard, put his hand up in front of the animal's face and said, "Stay!" Dodger didn't move and Brady experienced renewed admiration for the trainer. And a bit of jealousy.

Dobbs walked over to him. "That's what comes from a dog not knowing his place in the scheme of things around here," he said. "In the daylight, that crazy pup is out here at the stables, then come evening, Angela gives him a bath in perfumed shampoo so he can sleep on a velvet pillow at the foot of her bed." Dodger hadn't moved, but was panting with excitement, probably anticipating his next opportunity to sneak back to the stalls. "You don't know where you belong, do you, boy?" Dobbs said. He clucked his tongue a few times at Amber Mac and coaxed the animal to the door. "He's acting skittish. I think it's more than Dodger bothering him."

"He's probably hungry." With a slow, deliberate motion, Brady lifted his hand to stroke the thoroughbred's nose. "Time for lunch, fella."

Mac jerked his head out of reach.

"Okay, so we're not best friends yet."

Dobbs handed Brady a feed bucket. "He's only getting a pound of oats," Dobbs said. "He's been on grass and doesn't need any more than that."

Brady poured the oat pellets into the feed bucket. The horse immediately began to eat.

"Let's leave him be," Dobbs said, motioning for Brady to follow him. "Don't get discouraged. This is only his first full day at Cross Fox. He needs a good week or two to adjust to his new environment, even if these are the luxury accommodations."

Brady stopped halfway to the house and looked back. Dobbs turned to see what had caught his eye. The stables, built of brick and pine, stretched in a U-shaped arc with a stone statue of a thoroughbred in the center. Dutch doors opened onto each twelve-by-twelve stall. In the summer, when temperatures soared above ninety degrees, fans circulated continuously, keeping the horses cool and flies at bay.

Two full-time grooms cleaned brushes and kept the horses' coats glossy. A pair of stable hands washed feed buckets and mucked stalls twice a day. An industrial washing machine was constantly running, keeping blankets, bandages and wraps sanitary. The Cross Fox gardener manicured the lawn around the stable until it resembled a putting green and kept oak planters in front of each stall. This month they were still filled with the brilliant red poinsettias of the holiday season. Marshall spared no expense.

Amber Mac's accommodations were the best of the best. His stall opened onto a private paddock so he could come and go at will, allowing him the exercise needed to trim to an acceptable weight.

Brady crossed his arms and watched as Mac, finished with his meal, trotted into the paddock and stood with his head over the fence. "He's got it pretty good."

Dobbs started to comment but the sound of a car's laboring engine interrupted him. "You expecting company?"

"Not me." Brady peered down the half-mile drive. A rolling speck of white approached in a cloud of dust. "Who do we know who drives a tiny foreign thing like that?" he asked Dobbs.

"Nobody I can think of."

But suddenly Brady knew. Strands of dark brown hair whipped from the driver's window. George Strait blared from the radio. "Uh, Dobbs?"

"Yeah?"

"Do you remember seeing that car in Cliff's parking lot?"

The car stopped two-thirds of the way around

the circular drive, just past the entrance to the house. "Damn, Brady," he said. "That sure looks like our Molly."

"Shit, no, it can't be." Brady pushed his hat back from his forehead. "Sweet mercy, Dobbs, it's her. And she's got somebody else in the car."

Molly shut off the engine. Dust settled over the car, turning the faded exterior a gritty beige. She raked her fingers through her mussed hair, gathered it into a bunch and deftly wound some sort of band around it. She stepped out of the car and leaned an elbow on the top. "You told me not to wait too long," she said. "I guess this should be quick enough for you."

He tried to think of something to say, but his head was filled with the chug of her car as it came up the drive and the snorts of amusement coming from Dobbs. Not to mention the appearance of a woman who looked entirely different from the demure waitress in a red dress. This Molly filled out a pair of jeans about as well as anyone could. Her long-sleeved blouse opened at her neck revealing a turquoise charm dipping from a silver chain all the way down between… He looked up like a kid caught with his eyes on a centerfold.

She stepped away from the car and smoothed her hands down the sides of her jeans. "Aren't you going to say something?"

"You could have called first," he said, and resisted the urge to slap his hand against his forehead before something else equally inane came from his mouth.

"I didn't think it was necessary. We pretty well sealed the deal yesterday."

Had they? Well, yeah, he supposed she was right. But he hadn't expected her to actually show up. Yet here she was, standing in his driveway, her car loaded to the tops of its windows with stuff. And something else. He pointed. "Who's in the car?"

She leaned into the driver's window. "You can get out, Sammy. It's okay. This is the place I told you about."

The passenger door opened and a kid emerged, his sneakers crunching on the fine white gravel of the Carricks' drive. He stood there, the brim of a Dallas Mavericks ball cap shadowing his eyes and nose. A worn cotton horse, its hind legs squeezed in the kid's fist, dangled beside him. In the other hand, he gripped a plastic Slurpee cup. A T-shirt emblazoned with Prairie Bend Elementary School hung to the knees of a pair of husky-sized jeans.

Molly hurried around the car and put her hand on the boy's shoulder. "Say hi to Mr. Carrick and Mr. Dobbs."

The horse jerked upward, its front legs wiggling. "Hi."

"This is my son," she explained, as if it made perfect sense for her to descend on Cross Fox Ranch with family in tow. "His name is Sam."

Dobbs stepped forward and grinned at the kid. "Hello, Sam."

Brady acknowledged him with a nod. A silence

which might have become uncomfortable was broken by Dodger. The dog darted around Dobbs and ran at the kid, barking excitedly and wagging his stub of a tail.

Molly yanked the boy behind her. "Keep the dog back, will you?"

Brady released a snort of laughter. "That dog's not going to bite."

"I don't know that."

Dobbs called Dodger back and did his magic hand thing again to quiet the animal.

Brady stared at Molly. "I thought you said you didn't have any family."

"I believe I said I wasn't leaving behind anyone that matters. That's true. I brought Sam with me."

"A kid isn't part of the deal."

She settled her hand on Sam's ball cap. "No, he isn't."

"But how…?"

"You let me worry about that. It's not your problem."

"Like hell—" She scowled at him, and he clamped his mouth shut.

"If you'd like to discuss this later, I'd be happy to," she said. "Now's not the time."

If ever a man felt like he was being railroaded, this was it. When Brady got up that morning, he never thought he'd be trying to figure out what to make of Molly. He never believed he'd actually end up teaching her the ins and outs of poker. And he never figured that if she did show, she'd bring a carload of baggage that included a lot more than a few suitcases of clothes.

Brady reached in his back pocket and took out his wallet. "What'd it cost you to get here, Molly? I wouldn't want you to make the drive back today so here's enough for a motel room and dinner tonight. There's a nice place in town..."

She took a couple of steps toward him. "I don't want traveling expenses. I want the lessons. That's what you told me I'd get."

He frowned. "That was yesterday. And you brought a lot more to the table than you ever told me about, so why don't you take the money, head on back to Prairie Bend and we'll call the whole thing off."

She breathed deeply and spoke so low he had to lean in to hear her. That damn silver chain glinted in the sunlight and he had to remind himself to keep his eyes off it. "Okay," she said, "maybe I should have told you about Sam."

"You think?"

"But if I had, you wouldn't have offered me the deal."

"Damn straight."

She rolled her eyes to Sam. "Language."

Somehow he reined in his temper. "Why don't you take Molly's son for a walk?" he said to Dobbs.

"Sure. I can do that."

It was a great plan in theory, only the kid wouldn't budge. "Sit in the car, honey," she said to him. He got inside and sucked on the Slurpee.

Molly turned back to Brady. "Look, I'm sorry about blindsiding you, but Sam's going to start school soon. And when he's not in school, he won't be any trouble. He's a well-behaved boy. I will need to spend time with him, of course, but I'm sure you and I will find all the opportunities we need to study." Sensing he wasn't convinced, she added, "And I'm a fast learner. Really, I am. And I want to do this. I'm prepared to study hard and listen to everything you tell me."

He slanted a suspicious look at her. "Just exactly why do you want to learn poker, Molly? What do you want the money for?"

She parroted the line he'd given her the day before. "It's personal."

"I didn't get away with saying that yesterday," he said. "Why should I let you get away with it today?"

"You don't need to know," she evaded. "I did need to have answers about your motives. I'm the one taking a chance. I'm the outsider."

"You've got to give me something, Molly."

"I need a fresh start." She stared intently at him, like she'd done when they first met in the diner. "All you need to know is that when this is over, I'll leave. Like you explained yesterday, win or lose, I'll be out of your life. I give you my word."

Her word? What did Brady know about the word of a woman he'd just met? And yet he believed what she was saying. Unfortunately, believing did not mean he was ready to take on the responsibility of a newly unemployed waitress and her silent, overweight kid.

"What's going on out here?" Marshall's booming voice captured everyone's attention. He strode out the front door, crossed the veranda and came down the steps. Stopping at the edge of the drive, he looked at the overstuffed vehicle that Brady had now identified as an older model Honda, bent to check out the boy inside and turned his focus to the three adults several yards away. He thrust his hands on his hips and said, "Damn, if you didn't show up after all."

"Hello, Mr. Carrick."

He jutted a thumb at the car. "Is the kid yours?"

"He is."

He shook his head. "Double damn."

Molly glanced at the car. "Please, Mr. Carrick, can't you men say anything without swearing?"

He touched the brim of his hat. "Begging your pardon." He focused on Brady. "I guess the bet's in full swing now, isn't it, son?"

Brady frowned. "We're still working out the details. I wasn't exactly prepared for their arrival."

"You shoulda' been. She told you she was coming."

"Yes, but I thought she was just... Besides, I didn't know she'd have a..." The boy was staring out the window, probably hearing every word.

"He's just a tyke," Marshall said. "I can't see that he'll be much trouble."

Molly's shoulders relaxed. "Thank you, Mr. Carrick. That's exactly what I tried to tell your son."

The front door opened again, and Angela appeared in a long flowing dressing gown with ostrich feathers fluttering at the hem and the ends of the sleeves. "I heard a car," she said. "Do we have company?"

"Mom, this is Molly," Brady said as she floated down the steps. "I met her yesterday. She's come to work with me on a special project."

Angela blinked rapidly several times. "What kind of project?"

"Has to do with poker," Brady said.

Angela put her index finger to her bottom lip and stared at Molly. "How interesting. I'm sure you'll give me more details later, won't you, Brady?"

"Sure."

"What's your last name, dear?"

Molly turned away from Brady and answered Angela's question. His mother's small mouth rounded with interest. "Are you related to the Davises from King William Street in San Antonio?" she asked.

"No, ma'am. My maiden name is Whelan and I come from a small town outside Dallas."

"I'm sure that's nice, too." Angela stared over Molly's shoulder at the Honda. "Who's in the car?"

"That's my son, Sam."

"What an angelic face," Angela said. Brady didn't know how she'd come to that conclusion, since he couldn't see anything but the boy's mouth and plastic straw from where he stood.

Angela turned to Brady. "Where are these people staying, dear? And for how long?"

Brady fumbled for a response. "A few weeks, maybe," he said, still uncertain as to whether or not that was true. "And I don't know where they'll stay. They just got here."

Angela looked at Dobbs. "Have you hired a new stable foreman yet, Trevor?"

"No, ma'am."

"Perfect. Molly and Sam can stay in the apartment over the tack room." She looked at Brady and noted his less than enthusiastic reaction. "What's wrong? The apartment was recently refurbished. It's convenient if you'll be working together."

How could he tell his mother that her impulsive suggestion was just another example of the way her mind had been working lately. Since he'd come home from Vegas, Angela either approached situations with misplaced enthusiasm or bland indifference. He would have preferred indifference today. "I think we should let Molly decide," he said.

Chastised, her pale lips pulled into a frown, Angela murmured, "Of course."

They both looked at Molly. "I think it's a very generous offer," she said. "I'm sure Sam and I could be comfortable there."

Angela smiled. "Good. It's settled." She gathered the excess folds of her robe around her slim waist. "I'm going in now. I need coffee. Is breakfast being served in the conservatory?"

Marshall took her arm. "I'm afraid you've missed breakfast, Angela. You'll have to settle for a late lunch."

As they went toward the front entrance, Brady

heard his mother ask, "What time is it, Marsh? I can't imagine it's much past nine."

His answer was muffled as he led her inside.

Brady scrubbed his hand over the nape of his neck and looked at Molly. "So, do you want to see the apartment?"

"Sure. Thanks."

"You can drive around to the front of the stables. I'll meet you there."

As he turned away from her, he heard Dobbs say, "Welcome aboard, Molly. I think you'll like it here."

It occurred to Brady that he hadn't yet said anything remotely welcoming to Molly. And he was a long way from doing so. He had no idea what her angle was but he was certain that a woman who gave up everything to follow a crazy bet had to have one.

CHAPTER FOUR

SAM SAT ON THE LEATHER SOFA in the apartment above the tack room and channel-surfed the seemingly unending selection of television programs. "Wow, Mom," he said. "This is the neatest TV. It's huge."

Molly came out of the bedroom where she'd been storing their clothes in twin knotty pine dressers. "It sure is," she said, admiring the high-definition picture on the thirty-two inch flat-screen set. Her father's TV got fifteen channels and operated with an antenna fashioned out of two crooked rabbit ears wrapped in aluminum foil.

Sam settled on a Western movie with cowboys galloping across a rugged prairie. Reaching for his Coke, he said, "This whole place is so cool."

"Be sure you put the glass back on the coaster," Molly advised. "Otherwise you'll leave a mark on the table." She agreed with Sam's evaluation of their living quarters, but was trying not to appear overly impressed. After all, they'd be leaving all this behind in a few weeks. She didn't know why the Carricks no longer had a stable foreman, but it couldn't have been because he had a complaint about his apartment.

The living room was furnished with a butter-soft sofa and two brown leather chairs flanking a solid cherry coffee table. A game table and matching barrel chairs sat against a burgundy-painted wall. The pictures above it were typical Texas: prints of longhorn steer, fields of cattle, the capitol building in Austin. Each was framed to match the geometric rugs on the light maple floor.

The kitchen, with its expansive windows and white shutters, was a dream. Molly examined the top-of-the-line brushed-steel appliances, the hand-painted ceramic counters and the heavy oak dinette on the burnt-sienna Mexican-tile floor, imagining her uncle Cliff's reaction. He would have given a week's profit to prepare one meal in this state-of-the-art environment.

But the most pleasant surprise was the bedroom. A king-sized bed with a rustic four-post frame dominated the center of the room. It was covered in a plush Navajo spread, which matched the drapes on the two windows. A walk-in closet had built-in shelves where Molly was able to store Sam's toys. Molly especially loved the window that looked out on the suede green lawn. She could picture herself reading for hours here with the sunlight streaming in.

She sat next to Sam on the sofa and pretended to watch the movie. "I can't even imagine what the Carricks' house must be like on the inside," she said after a moment.

Sam looked up at her with wide brown eyes. "It can't be any better than this one."

She smiled. She couldn't imagine Marshall Carrick or his son, Brady, designing the Victorian with gabled roofs, whimsical cupolas and stained-glass casement windows. She'd only been acquainted with Angela Carrick for a few brief moments, but she believed the willowy woman in ostrich feathers, with her wavy blond hair and those long thin fingers that seemed made to play a piano, was the mastermind behind the Carrick house. If that were so, why did the nervous woman seem out of place in an environment that must once have suited her so perfectly?

"Mama, I'm hungry."

Deep in thought, Molly hadn't realized that Sam had shut off the television. She glanced at the clock on the mantelpiece. "Goodness. It's nearly seven o'clock. You must be starved." She went into the kitchen and examined the refrigerator where she'd put the few items she'd brought in a cooler from Prairie Bend. "We still have some sandwiches left. And chips and cookies. How does that sound?"

"I'm sick of sandwiches," he said.

"Then we can go to the convenience store we passed when we drove out here. I can get a frozen pizza."

"Okay."

She grabbed her purse, bundled Sam into his jacket and headed for the door. Opening it, she nearly ran into a plump dark-haired Mexican woman on the threshold. She carried a platter covered with a checkered cloth, and whatever was under the napkin smelled spicy and hot and heavenly. Molly's mouth watered. "Hi."

"Hello," the woman said. "Can I come in? I'm Serafina, Trevor Dobbs's wife."

Molly opened the door wider. "It's nice to meet you, Serafina."

"How do like this place?" Serafina asked as she took the platter to the kitchen.

"It's lovely."

"I'm having another bed brought up tomorrow," she said. "It's a folding one, but has a nice thick mattress. It will be good for the boy."

"Thank you. That's very thoughtful."

She placed the platter on the table. Sam followed her as if she were the pied piper. "What's under that napkin?" he asked.

Serafina smiled. "I thought you might be hungry, *niño.* I've brought you some supper."

"How kind of you," Molly said. "But we don't want to be any trouble."

"It's no trouble," Serafina assured her. "And it's not much. During the week we eat simple food." She removed the cloth, releasing deliciously scented steam, and pointed to the various offerings on the plate. "Some tacos, enchiladas, beans, corn. It should be enough for you and the boy."

Molly didn't need to ask, but she said, "What do you think, Sam? Does it look good?"

"It looks great." He began rooting through

drawers. "Where are the forks?" When he found them, he sat at the table and waited for Molly to bring him the last of the milk from the nearly empty refrigerator.

"Thank you so much, Serafina," Molly said. "You're a lifesaver."

"I just saw your supplies in that ice box," she said. "You come to the main house in the morning and get whatever you need." She frowned at the refrigerator. "I will take you shopping tomorrow."

"I'd like that."

"If you need me, we live in the smaller house just to the west. You come get me."

Molly walked her to the door. Serafina stopped before going out. "One more thing."

"Yes?"

"Mr. Brady told me to tell you he would be up later for your first lesson." She shook her head. "Poker, is it?"

Not knowing what this woman knew of her arrangement with Brady or, if she did, whether or not she approved of it, Molly hesitated before answering, "Yes, it's poker."

Serafina waved her hand in a dismissive gesture. "I guess Brady knows poker. At least that's what they all say—Trevor and those friends of his. But I told him you must be tired and he should let you settle in tonight."

Serafina was frowning because she was concerned about Molly's welfare? Having grown up with criticism as part of her everyday life, Molly laughed with relief. "It's okay. I'm always up late. Tell him to come."

Serafina started down the stairs. "Go. Eat. You're too skinny. And tell Brady to leave when you tire of him. He could play poker all night."

Molly shut the door and leaned against it. Just a few minutes ago, she'd been as hungry as Sam. Now, her appetite seemed to have fled.

"This is what you want, Molly," she said, anticipating the satisfaction of soaking up every bit of knowledge Brady had to give her. A big payoff. And revenge. She was glad she'd come to River Bluff. Brady would teach her all the tricks he'd used to humiliate Kevin, only she'd be the winner this time. She imagined Brady's face when she finally revealed her identity to him. In the back of her mind, she could almost see Kevin grinning.

MOLLY ONLY NIBBLED at the food Serafina brought. When she'd cleaned up the dishes, she showered, tamed her hair into a loose style that fell around her shoulders and slipped into comfortable running pants and a sweatshirt. A thermometer outside the door of the apartment read forty-two degrees, uncharacteristically cool for south central Texas, even in the winter.

She tucked Sam into bed at eight-thirty and sat on the sofa to find something entertaining on television. She was staring at a reality show when her half-hearted concentration was broken by a knock at the door. The knowledge that Brady was supposed to begin her lessons had never really left her mind and she jumped up from the sofa. Her hand on the knob, she gave herself a quick pep talk. "Calm down, Molly. This is a business arrangement, an opportunity for both of you to get what you want. Don't blow it."

She opened the door. Brady stood on her small landing, two bottles of beer dangling between his fingers. He wore jeans, sneakers and a flannel shirt under a black leather jacket. His damp hair glistened, and he smelled faintly of pine and something subtly spicy. "Is this a bad time?" he asked.

She stood back. "No. Come in."

He strode to the middle of the room, set the beer on the coffee table and pulled out a deck of cards. "Accommodations okay?"

"Fine."

"I figured we might as well get started."

"Sure."

From the bedroom, Sam called out, "Mom? Who's here?"

"Uh-oh," Brady said. "Looks like I woke the kid."

"He wasn't asleep yet." She stuck her head in the bedroom door. "It's Mr. Carrick, honey. Everything's fine."

"Which Mr. Carrick? The one who swears?"

"Tough question," Brady said. "We both do."

"The younger one, Brady," she said.

"Oh, okay. G'night."

She smiled as she shut the door. "He's tired from traveling."

Brady shrugged out of his jacket without commenting. He tossed it over the back of the sofa and walked to the game table. "You want to turn that thing off?" he said, pointing to the television.

She hit the remote's power button. He sat at the table and indicated the opposite chair. "Have a seat. We'll just go over some basics tonight."

She sat. "Okay."

He pulled the cards from the box and shuffled. She couldn't help noticing his hands. For a rich guy, they were surprisingly calloused and his nails were short and squared off.

She imagined those hands reaching out to catch a football. Kevin had never missed a Dallas game if he was home and not at a rodeo event. Brady Carrick had been one of his favorites. She tried to remember what position he'd played. Wide receiver, she thought. Kevin had certainly idolized him. She'd never quite understood the fascination. She'd never been much of a football fan, but Kevin had been so excited when he called her from Las Vegas that fateful night saying he'd met the great Brady Carrick in person.

He flicked on a floor lamp beside the table, flooding the inlaid wood with bright light. Then he spread the cards in a perfect arc across the top. "Fifty-two cards in a deck," he said. "And two jokers."

"I know what's in a deck of cards," she said, though she'd only become acquainted with them at friends' homes and from Kevin after she was married.

He half smiled. "Most people do. But there's a lot of Bible Belt Baptists up where you come from, so a guy can't take anything for granted."

An image of her father popped into her mind and she flinched. Brady Carrick couldn't know how right he was about her background.

He pulled one card from each suit out of the deck. "There are four suits, thirteen cards in each."

"I *know.* You can skip the simple stuff."

"Okay." He stood up, went to the coffee table and twisted the cap off a beer. He held the other bottle out to her. "Want one?"

"No thanks."

He came back, took a swig and started to set the bottle down. She immediately reached for a coaster and put it under the beer. He paused, grinned and slipped two sixes from the deck. "This is a pair. A pair is sometimes a decent poker hand, but the higher the number, the better, through the face cards to the aces. Wired aces, what poker players call a pair in the hole, are the best. But any pair is usually enough to bet with."

She reached over and pulled out another six. "Three of a kind. Even better."

"Right."

She located the last six and put it with the other three. "Obviously..."

"Yeah. Four of a kind, also known as quads. It's a darn good hand, almost always a winner."

"I would think so," she said.

He proceeded to show her other winning combinations, ending with a royal flush. "Do you know the statistical chances of getting one of these in a five-card Texas Hold 'Em hand?" he asked her.

She really wanted to respond, so she tried to come up with a logical answer. Math had been her best subject in high school and junior college. Fifty-two cards, permutations numbering in the hundreds of thousands... After a moment her mind began to buzz and she gave up. "No," she admitted.

"One in about thirty-one thousand."

She smiled. "So I want to get a lot of those."

"Well, yeah, but since you probably won't, you've got to know how to use these other combinations to your best advantage."

"Okay, show me."

He snapped the cards up and reshuffled. "I'm going to start by teaching you the basics of Texas Hold 'Em poker." He laid two cards in front of her and two in front of himself, all face up. "You said you've watched the game on TV?"

"A few times."

"Good. Imagine that these two cards are the ones dealt face down to each player at the beginning of each hand. They're called the hole cards." He flipped three more cards from the deck. "After the first round of betting, these next three are dealt. They're called the flop and are placed in the center, face up. Each player at the table gets to use them to make his hand. As well as—" he turned over a card "—the fourth card, called the turn, and—" he flipped another one "—a fifth card, known as the river."

Brady looked up at her, held her gaze for a moment and then cleared his throat. He pointed to the cards in front of her. "Remember, you're the only one who knows what your hole cards are. You make your first bet based on what you were dealt. And, whatever you do, don't let any other player at the table guess what you might have by a change in your facial expression."

She studied Brady's face now. No wonder he was so good at this game. She could swear that the intensity of his stare had nothing to do with his enthusiasm for the game. He seemed to be analyzing her, not the cards. Maybe that was his strategy. If so, it was certainly unnerving. She crossed her legs and then uncrossed them, but couldn't get comfortable.

Two hours later, Brady had knocked back both beers, but it was Molly who felt dizzy. She'd offered to get a tablet to take notes but he'd stopped her. "No notes. This has to be second nature. If you don't get it the first time, we'll go over it again. Having it on paper isn't what counts." He pointed to the side of his head. "It's got to be in here." He stood up. "We're done for tonight."

She picked up the bottles and carried them into the kitchen. "How'd I do?" she asked when she returned and met him at the door.

"Not bad."

It wasn't the answer she had hoped for. *Spectacular* or at least *pretty well* would have been better, but she'd have to be satisfied with *not bad.* She went outside with him and watched him descend the steps to ground level. "Brady?"

He stopped, turned around.

"You're not angry with me anymore?"

He stared up at her for a long moment. Just before the silence became uncomfortable, he said, "You pulled a fast one and you know it. But you're here. We made a deal and I'm not going to back out."

She went back inside and watched him out the window. "I guess I won't get any Texas-style gallantry from you."

"DAMN. Damn it. What the hell is going on here?" Brady muttered as he kicked clods of dirt ahead of his footsteps. It felt good to finally vent his frustration without being censured by piercing blue eyes that could make a man feel like he was coated with frost one minute and melting into a puddle the next. His insides were as tight as the cinch on a newly broke saddle pony. He rolled his shoulders, locked his hands behind his back and stretched. Nothing helped.

Now he knew why many men, smarter than he, avoided teaching anything to a woman, especially one that had even a fraction of the appeal of this determined waitress from Prairie Bend. Take driving. A smart man would know better than to try and keep his mind on gears and pedals after confining himself to the front seat of an automobile with a sexy woman. A smart man would know better than to teach a soft, curvy woman to play golf knowing he'd end up spoon-curled behind her with his hands on her arms in the pretense of showing her how to swing. And a smart man *should* know better than to teach a woman poker, if it meant staring at her over a mere thirty-six inches of tabletop.

Every time Molly chewed on her bottom lip, Brady ended up honing in on the moisture that glistened on the soft flesh when she was finished. Each time she sighed in concentration and her breasts rose and fell, taking that damn turquoise charm farther into its cozy nest, he felt her warm breath in the blood rushing to places that had nothing to do with a discussion of odds and wagers.

But despite the temptations he hadn't counted on, he'd done what he had to do and there was comfort and pride in that. He'd kept Molly in her place, let her think this whole bet was completely in his control. He'd made her believe he was keeping his pledge out of a sense of honor, nothing more. And he was, wasn't he? A Carrick's word was his bond. Marshall had pounded that into him since he'd first learned to walk. If he hadn't given his word to Molly in the parking lot of Cliff's Diner, he would have sent her and her chubby-cheeked kid back to Prairie Bend.

When he reached the house and opened the back door, he remembered his father's warning to him when he'd left two hours ago. "Those people are your responsibility now, Brady. You brought them here. Sometimes we discover we don't want the responsibility we've bargained for, but it's ours nevertheless. You've got to do the right thing by this gal."

He caught his reflection in the refrigerator door. "You stupid ass." He reached for a beer and then changed his mind and settled for a cherry cola before collapsing at the kitchen table. More times than he cared to admit, his father had made him hate the word *responsibility.* He'd felt responsible every time he'd dropped a pass; when he'd zigged instead of zagged and busted his knee; when his marriage had failed; when he'd blown tons of money gambling; and, worst of all, when he'd met that cocky rodeo cowboy in Vegas. He'd felt responsible for all of that.

He supposed his father's lessons in responsibility had made him a better man, but now, when he was starting over, all he really wanted to do was think about a horse. Forty-eight hours ago, Amber Mac had consumed his life. Then he'd gone for a hamburger in Prairie Bend.

CHAPTER FIVE

THOUGH FURNISHED with every modern convenience, the kitchen in the Carrick house still had a Victorian ambiance. Sitting at the large pine table in the middle of the room, Molly admired the old-world charm of tiled counters designed with sprigs of violets and ivy, huge porcelain sinks with chrome spigots and a warm brick floor stained the color of cinnamon.

On this Saturday morning, January nineteenth, the room was alive with women working. Having finished sorting numerous tenderizers and seasonings into groups, Ruby had gone to the butcher shop to pick up her order of pork and beef, leaving Serafina and Molly under twin ceiling fans that circulated tempting aromas of hot spices. Serafina, whose specialty was Southwestern dishes, had begun making gallons of salsa at sunrise. She scooped fresh cilantro into a mixing bowl half filled with serrano peppers, tomatoes and onions. Wiping her hands on herapron, she came over to Molly, who'd started slicing avocados.

"How am I doing?" Molly asked, tapping the seed in a plump fruit with the side of her paring knife.

"Fine. But the pit will come out easier if you stick the knife underneath it and twist." She demonstrated with a quick turn of her wrist.

Molly did as the Mexican woman suggested, and the large seed popped out of the soft avocado center. "Wow, it worked."

Serafina chuckled. "You sound surprised, *cariño,* but I've had a lot of practice making guacamole."

Molly scooped the fruit from the shell with a spoon and diced it. She paused before picking up her fork to mash them, stood and went to the kitchen window.

"Do you see Sam and Trevor?" Serafina asked.

"Yes. Sam's still tossing a stick for Dodger, and Dobbs is going about his business with one eye on the stables and one on my son. I hope Sam isn't too much trouble for him."

"Don't worry. Trevor is pleased to have a *muchacho* around again. Our two daughters and their children live in Austin and we don't see them often enough." She smiled. "Sam seems to be having fun with the dog."

"Once he and Dodger got acquainted yesterday, that pup was all he talked about." Molly returned to the table and started mashing. "Except for the horses. He really wants to get close to the horses."

"Dobbs won't let him near the large animals without your permission."

Molly was relieved. She didn't want anyone at

Cross Fox to misinterpret Sam's enthusiasm for experience—not the kindly Dobbs nor the overly confident Brady. But Brady hadn't shown any interest in her son, so what was she worried about? In fact, he probably still resented her bringing Sam to the ranch.

She'd only caught glimpses of Brady yesterday. Serafina said he'd been running errands for Marshall's birthday preparations.

Pushing Brady from her mind, she concentrated on the avocado. Showing the results of her work to Serafina, she asked, "Okay?"

"Perfect." She smiled. "Now, all we need is about two dozen mashed that way and we'll have enough. Once you've finished, add chili powder and lemon juice and mix it thoroughly."

Molly reached for the next piece of fruit.

"I appreciate you coming today," Serafina said. "I would have had to hire a girl from River Bluff to help me get things ready if you hadn't volunteered."

"I'm happy to do it. I need something to keep me busy." She popped the pit from another avocado and repeated the process. "Can I ask you a question, Serafina?"

"Of course. Anything."

"I need to apply for a job, even if it's only for the few weeks I'll be here. Do you know of any restaurants in town that might be hiring?"

"The restaurants in town are always looking for help," Serafina said. "Despite this being a small town, the population is transient. People come and they go." She continued to chop vegetables. "What is it you want to do? Are you a cook?"

Molly laughed. "Seeing me in the kitchen today, I know you don't believe that. I've been working as a waitress."

"And that's what you want to do here?"

There wasn't any point in telling Serafina that she dreaded the thought of serving more burgers and fries to cowboys, but what else was there in a small town for a woman with two years' worth of junior college and ten years' experience waiting tables? "It's fine," she said. "I'm a good waitress."

Serafina listed a few places in town, and Molly committed them to memory. "I can put in a word for you with Ed Falconetti, the owner of The Longhorn Café," Serafina said. "All the men around here eat at the place and Ed sometimes plays in Brady's poker games."

"I'd really appreciate that," Molly said.

The women worked in silence for a few minutes until Serafina said, "Have you ever done anything else besides work in a restaurant?"

"Not really. I studied math in community college, but never got my degree. I'm pretty good with numbers."

Serafina's chopping knife stilled. "You know bookkeeping?"

"The basics, yes. I'm familiar with most of the widely used computer accounting programs."

Serafina scurried to a pantry closet, wiping her hands

on her apron. She withdrew a ledger and carried it to the table. She opened it to reveal numbers organized into neat columns. "Can you make sense of this?"

Molly stared at the simple double-entry bookkeeping, a basic checks-and-balances system. She looked up at Serafina. "This isn't difficult at all."

"Maybe so," Serafina said, "but nobody around here seems to have an interest in keeping our records straight. Even Brady, the fancy college graduate, doesn't want to get our books ready to turn into the ranch accountant."

"Someone's been doing them," Molly said. "I'd have to study this, of course, but the totals appear to match, adding across and up and down."

"Our stable foreman kept these," Serafina said. "But he's gone." She opened a drawer in the pantry and scooped dozens of scraps of paper into her hands. "These are just a few of the ranch receipts from the last month. Nobody has entered them, and they keep piling up."

"I'll be happy to take a look," Molly said. "If it'll help you out."

Serafina tossed the scraps back into the drawer. "Help me out? Molly, if you can account for all these receipts, you will help me sleep at night!"

Molly laughed. "I'm sure I can find time when I'm not working with Brady. Even after I get a job in town…"

Flattening her palm against her chest, Serafina said, "Forget that! You're working here. I just hired you."

The back door slammed and Brady came through the mudroom door. He set a carton on the table and stared first at Molly and then Serafina. He didn't look happy. "What's going on? Serafina, what have you hired Molly to do?"

MOLLY STARED AT HIM as if he were the last person she'd expected to see. A strange reaction considering this was his house and she was sitting in his kitchen…with mashed avocado on her fingers. Serafina immediately picked up a Cross Fox ledger from the table and held it under his nose.

"She's our new bookkeeper."

Molly blushed to the roots of her hair. "Well, nothing's been decided yet."

"Of course it has," Serafina said. "Do you really want to work in a diner in a town full of roughneck cowboys? Some of the men around here expect waitresses to serve up more than bowls of chili."

Realizing he was the only one in the room who didn't know what was going on, Brady stepped between the two women. "Who said anything about Molly working in a diner?"

"She did," Serafina answered. "She asked me for names of places that might be hiring."

He glared at Molly. "What for? I'm covering your rent."

Serafina nodded. "You tell her, Brady. The idea is loco. Especially when she can take that drawer full of papers and make sense of them."

"What makes you think she can do that?" Brady asked Serafina.

A sharp rap on the table silenced both of them. Molly stood with both hands flat on the tabletop. "I'm in the room, for heaven's sakes. The two of you don't have to talk about me as if I'm not."

Serafina managed a repentant grin. "Sorry."

"Fine," Brady said. "So tell me what brought this on."

Molly blew out a long breath. "First of all, I didn't agree to take on the responsibility of the Cross Fox books. I said I'd help that's all."

Serafina clasped her hands over her breasts and gave her a supplicating look. "But you will, won't you?" She thrust a finger at Brady. "This one won't do it. I've asked Mr. Marshall and Angela and neither one of them is interested. And Trevor…bah! The only numbers he knows is how many minutes it takes a horse to run a quarter mile."

"That would be seconds," Brady corrected. "Dobbs wouldn't spend much time on a horse that needs minutes to run the quarter."

He let his cocky smile fade from his face when Serafina gave him an all-too-familiar threatening scowl. More than once over the years he'd run out of the house just ahead of Serafina's broom and he wisely sensed his smart remark wasn't earning him brownie points now.

Ignoring the tension between Brady and Serafina, Molly continued. "Secondly, yes, you furnished Sam and me with a place to live and I'm grateful, but we have expenses beyond rent. There's food…and other necessities. Sam will need things for school starting Monday."

"And you thought you'd hire out at a dive in town?" Brady decided that later on, he'd have to sort out just exactly why that idea bothered him so much.

"What's wrong with that?" Molly said. "You found me in a dive, didn't you?"

"That's different. You work for me now. It's my bet."

She jutted her chin out. "Yes, it's your bet, but that doesn't mean you can make decisions for me. Besides, the way I look at it, I don't work for you. I work with you."

"For? With? That's just semantics."

"Not to me, it isn't."

"Then you'd better not take Serafina's offer to keep the books, because guess what? In reality, you'd be working for me."

"Then I quit."

Serafina swatted his arm and pushed him out of her way. "Don't listen to him, *cariño*. You're working for me." She gave him a warning look over her shoulder. "I hire for the household, not this cock-of-the-walk rooster who thinks he's the king of the henhouse."

Molly glared at him. Her chest rose and fell with each breath. Brady looked for the silver chain. She wasn't wearing it today or if she was, the charm was tucked underneath the rust-colored knit thing she had on, hiding somewhere warm and soft and out of bounds.

She narrowed her eyes as if she were trying to figure out which one of them she should trust. Brady was Marshall Carrick's son, but Serafina had been at the ranch longer than he'd been alive. He wouldn't want to bet on whose decisions carried the most weight inside this house.

"Fine," Molly said after a tension-filled moment. "I'll do the books while I'm here."

"And you'll forget about working in town," Brady said.

She agreed with a nod.

Serafina looked at the ceiling. *"Gracias a Dios."* The matter settled, Serafina examined the contents of the carton Brady had just deposited on the table. "Good. You got the ingredients for my special barbecue sauce."

"It's all here."

"Now you can call the party people and make sure they're bringing the canopies and chairs."

He was about to tell her that apparently cocky roosters were good for something when a scream erupted from the yard near the stables. Molly clutched her chest. "My God. That sounds like Sam."

She tore past him and out the back door. He followed, ignoring the pain in his leg as he caught up to her. He saw the kid sitting on the concrete slab supporting the horse statue, his knee pulled up to his chest, his head bent, eyes staring in terror. Dobbs jogged toward him from one of the stalls and Dodger stood nearby, a stick in his jaws.

Molly hit the concrete and dropped next to her son. "Sammy, what happened?" When she saw the tear in the kid's jeans and a trickle of blood running down his leg, she covered her mouth with her hand. "Oh, baby."

The kid howled and shrank into her arms.

Brady knelt beside him and examined the injury. As wounds went, he'd seen much worse.

Molly looked at him. "Should we call an ambulance?"

He blinked. "Not for him. Do you need one?"

"That's not funny."

"Sorry." He examined the kid's knee. "How'd you do this?"

Sam wiped his eye with a dirty finger. "I f-fell. I was r-running after Dodger and tripped."

Molly hugged him closer and stroked his hair. "Oh, Sam. That must hurt..."

"Your damn...darn pants are too long, kid," Brady said. "It's no wonder you tripped."

Molly gave him a scathing glare and started to say something he knew he wouldn't like. He held up a hand. "He's okay. It's a scrape. Probably needs a stitch or two."

"Stitches?" They both said the word as if his prognosis had been a quadruple bypass.

Brady stood, located Dobbs over his shoulder. "Get me some bandages and a bucket of water from the infirmary, will you?"

Molly sat up straight. "The stable infirmary? You're going to stop the bleeding with horse bandages?"

"A bandage is a bandage, Molly. They're washed and disinfected." Then, thinking it would calm her down, he said the worst thing he could have. "Believe me, I'd be a lot more concerned about a gash on a thoroughbred's leg than I am this scratch on the kid."

Her expression said, *how dare you, you horrible monster, get away from my son right now.* Brady tried to memorize it so he could use it on the guys at the next poker game. That kind of intimidation could work to his advantage.

When Serafina arrived on the golf cart, he figured he'd better try to defuse this situation or he'd have both women ganging up on him. He raised his hands in the air. "I'm sorry. That didn't come out exactly right…." Dobbs handed him clean bandages. Brady took one and pressed it to the knee.

Molly snatched it away. "I'll do it."

He watched with mounting impatience as she tentatively dabbed at the wound, which, he had to admit was bleeding more profusely now. Her hand shook so badly she wasn't accomplishing much. "You'd better let me do that," he said.

She released a ragged breath. Serafina put a hand on her shoulder and nodded. Brady took a clean bandage, dipped it in the bucket and wiped away the blood. Then he held the compress tightly against the wound. "Bring my truck around, okay, Dobbs?"

Molly gasped. "What for?"

"Like I said, he probably needs stitches. We're going into town to the clinic."

"I hope Becky's there," Serafina said as Dobbs took off in the cart. "She's a wonderful nurse. She'll take good care of Sam. Her father, Hub Parker, used to be sheriff of Bandera County," she added, as if it would make Molly feel better.

Brady tied another bandage around the blood-stained one and slid his hand under Sam's arm to help him to his feet. "It's going to be okay, you know that, don't you?"

He sniffled. "But it hurts."

"Well, yeah, knees are like that." He flexed his leg, easing the pain from being in a crouched position. "Trust me, I know." Turning to Molly, Brady said, "Do you need help getting up, Mom?"

"No. I'm fine."

She didn't appear fine. In fact, Brady had to point out to her that Dodger was licking avocado from her fingertips.

Dobbs pulled up in Brady's truck a minute later and Brady, Molly and Sam piled inside. "You'll hurry, won't you?" Molly said, her voice still edged with panic.

He sped down the half-mile drive and onto the two-lane blacktop that led to River Bluff.

Molly alternated between checking Sam in the backseat and eyeing her watch. "It's Saturday," she said. "Are you sure the clinic will be open?"

"Until noon," Brady said. "Besides, I told

Serafina to call and alert them we were coming. If they were going to close, she would have called me on my cell."

Molly twisted her fingers together, glanced in the back again. "How are you doing, Sammy?"

The kid sniffed, murmured a response Brady couldn't understand.

"I know it hurts, baby, but we'll be there soon."

Brady ground his teeth, a bad habit, but jeez, didn't Molly realize how she was coddling the kid? He checked in the rearview mirror. "You're doing fine, aren't you, Sam?" he said. "Tell your mother to quit worrying."

"I can't lie," he said. "It hurts."

Brady rolled his eyes. Cripes, the kid was making a mountain out of a molehill. Someday he'd have to tell him that men were supposed to buck up in front of their women, principles of truth and honesty be damned.

"Can't you drive any faster?" Molly said.

"Yes, I can, but I'm going five miles over the limit now and I'd rather not get a speeding ticket."

"It didn't seem this far between town and your ranch when we drove out here two days ago."

Brady stared straight ahead. "Well, I can guarantee you it was. Nobody added more miles to the trip in the past forty-eight hours."

He sensed her cold stare. "Are you always this sarcastic?" she asked.

"No. I can exhibit varying degrees of sarcasm. This is just one of them."

MOLLY HELD HER TEMPER by sheer force of will. Brady Carrick was an insensitive jerk. Didn't he have an ounce of compassion? Yes, he'd been competent back at the ranch, had handled the basics of tending to the wound well enough, better than she could have. But competency was only a fraction of what was needed in this situation. She wanted to scream, "Sam's only seven years old! Can't you cut him some slack in the sympathy department?"

But she kept silent and focused her attention on her son. She couldn't help drawing a conclusion about Brady and her husband. The two men, opposite in so many ways, were alike in one respect. Kevin had tried to make a man of Sam, too, and he and Molly often argued about her mothering techniques. He once criticized her for *smothering* instead of mothering. "Let the boy learn from his mistakes, Mol," he'd said to her. "Quit babying him."

But when Molly looked at her son, she didn't see the tough little guy Kevin tried to force into adulthood too soon. She saw a child who'd had to face the trials of a limited world he didn't create. A boy with a father who was gone for weeks at a time, and a mother who constantly worried about paying the bills. She battled guilt every day because Sam had to get by without so many of the things other kids had. He wore second-hand clothes, played with dollar-store toys and ate leftovers from Cliff's Diner at a kitchen table surrounded by buckets catching rainwater.

But Kevin always told her it wouldn't be like that

forever. One day he'd get the break he deserved. He'd win the big rodeo prize. And Molly believed him because she loved him. But she decided that until it happened, the one thing Sam wouldn't lack was his mother's love. Maybe she couldn't guarantee he'd be happy every minute of every day, but she could make sure he didn't have to grow up until he was ready.

She sighed with relief when she saw the outline of buildings just ahead. She'd only caught a glimpse of the River Bluff business district on Thursday before she'd turned onto the road that took them to Cross Fox. And she was much too nervous to care what the town was like today.

Sam grabbed her seat from behind. "Hey, Mom, see that?" He pointed out the window to power poles decorated with metal sculptures—cowboys on horseback, long-horned steer. "This is a neat place."

Molly darted a glance at Brady. He was smiling. She didn't know if that was a result of pride in his town or smugness that Sam had finally stopped carrying on about his injury. "Yes, it's very neat," she said. "We'll come back and have a look around, maybe Monday after school."

She noticed a sign on a storefront and read it to Sam, "River Bluff, Where the Wild West Is a Way of Life."

"Wow. Cool."

The buildings on both sides of Main Street did exude Old West. Some structures were made of native limestone, now aged and sun-bleached. Others appeared much like a movie set; false fronts buttressed from behind gave the impression of a typical 1880s Texas town.

The names of gift shops and specialty stores were colorful and appropriate. The Lazy Wrangler. The Cow Creek Shop. The Trading Post. The Cowboy Supply Store had a giant red boot on top. And of course, there were a few saloons with Western names and blinking neon beer signs in the windows. A water tower loomed with the town's name printed on the side, as well as the announcement that the River Bluff Broncos had once been state champs. When Brady put his blinker on, Molly asked, "How far is the clinic?"

"Just down this street two blocks."

"Great."

They pulled in front of a simple one-story building with the words *Family Clinic* on the window. For a moment Molly was disappointed. She'd half expected to see a two-story wood structure with stairs leading up the side to an office labeled simply Doc. Even her dad would have appreciated that detail. He watched reruns of *Gunsmoke* nearly every night.

The three got out of the truck and walked inside a clean, functional reception area. A young woman in cotton scrubs looked up from a book. "Can I help you?" She noticed Sam's stained, torn jeans and said, "I see why you're here." Sliding a clipboard across a counter, she added, "Just fill this out. Either one of you is fine, the mother or the father."

Molly grabbed the clipboard. "I'm his mother."

She nodded at Brady. "He's..." She fumbled for a description.

"A pain-in-the-ass friend?" he offered.

A door to the right of the registration area opened and a woman wearing a denim skirt, sneakers and a lab coat came out. She was petite and slim, with short auburn hair and expressive blue eyes. Molly estimated her to be about her own age. She smiled as she approached, her hand outstretched. "Hey, Brady, how are you?"

"Fine, Becky," he said. "You're looking as pretty as ever."

She dismissed his compliment with a wave. "Serafina called and said you'd be bringing in a patient." She got down on one knee in front of Sam. "I'm guessing this is the wounded cowboy right here."

"That's him."

"What's your name, honey?"

Sam told her and Brady cleared his throat. "This is his mother, Molly."

Becky stood to shake Molly's hand. "Hi. Good to meet you." Her palm felt warm, assuring. "You look pale," she said. "You want to sit down?"

"No. I'm fine."

Becky smiled. "This doesn't look too bad. Once I check under that bandage I'll know for sure, but the bleeding has stopped. That's a good sign. Who wrapped this?"

"Brady did," Molly said.

Becky grinned fondly. "Good job for a wide receiver, jock man."

He gave her a cocky smile, one that came across as teasing between two old friends. "All in a day's work, Beck."

"Let's go into the office." She led them through the door to an exam room and asked Sam to take his jeans off. Once he was on the table she unwrapped his knee. "How'd you do this, Sam?"

He told her a long, convoluted story about a dog, a stick, running real fast, tripping and sliding on "the stuff around the horse statue."

Becky listened intently while she cleaned and studied the injury. "Wow. What happened to the dog?"

Sam laughed. "Nothing. He's okay."

"This is going to heal fine," she said to Molly, "but I'm advising a few stitches. That way Sam won't have much of a scar and we'll reduce the chance of infection if the cut should open again. I know how boys can be when we tell them not to roughhouse for a few days."

Molly had trusted this woman the moment she knelt in front of Sam, and her trust had only grown in the past few minutes. "Okay," she said. "What do you want me to do?"

Becky ruffled Sam's hair before walking to a supply cabinet. She took out a needle. "Just promise him some ice cream later. I'm going to give him an injection to anesthetize the area." To Sam she said, "You're going to feel a tiny pinprick from this, Sam. But it won't hurt when I do the stitches. Promise."

Sam looked up at Brady as if getting his opinion on the procedure. Brady sent him a nod of man-to-man encouragement. Sam pinched his eyes closed, sucked in a breath and said, "Do it."

Fifteen minutes later, Sam sported four stitches in his knee, a nice padding of gauze and the option to pick the flavor of ice cream he wanted.

"So whose heart are you breaking tonight, Becky?" Brady asked while Molly wrote a check for the expenses.

"Nobody's. I'll be renting a movie and buying a pizza. How about you?"

"Jake, Luke and I are coming into town. We'll probably hang out for a while and see what develops."

A shadow flitted across her eyes at the mention of the two men's names. Molly figured Becky knew at least one of them well. "How's Jake doing?" Becky asked. "I've only seen him once or twice since his uncle Verne's funeral and I know Rachel's back in town."

"Oh, yeah. Then you also know they're on their way to working things out this time," Brady said.

"Seems pretty clear to me," Becky said. "Those two belong together."

Brady leaned on the examination table. "So, Beck, why don't you come along tonight?"

"Are you kidding? If I know you three, you might just end up at the Scoot 'n Boot, and I'll have to give you stitches after you get in a brawl. Folks around here didn't call you guys the Wild Bunch for nothing."

"Hey, that's ancient history," he said, pretending

a boyish innocence, which made both women smirk. "We're not like that anymore."

She took Molly's check. "Right."

"Are you coming to the Carrick hoedown tomorrow?"

"No. I'll be here at the clinic doling out aspirins to our closest friends. My father will have to represent the Parker-Howard clan."

"Won't be the same without you. Dad's hired the Lonesome Coyote Band to play. Who'll I two-step with?"

She shook her head. "If that's the biggest problem you have, Brady Carrick, then you lead a charmed life."

Becky gave Molly a list of instructions to care for Sam's wound and they left the office. Once in the truck, Brady turned to Molly and said, "What are you doing tonight?"

What did he think she was doing? She was new in town, didn't know a soul except for the people at Cross Fox and, now, the local nurse. She frowned at him and said, "Don't forget to stop at the convenience store. My plans tonight include two pints of chocolate fudge ripple and I don't know what Sam wants."

CHAPTER SIX

NINE EMPTY ROCKS GLASSES sat in the middle of the table at the Scoot 'n Boot Saloon on Saturday night. Looking out the grimy window onto Main Street, Brady tried to ignore the earsplitting blast of country music from the jukebox.

A waitress attempted again to remove the empty glasses. "Leave 'em," Luke said. "How else are we going to know when we're drunk?"

Brady chuckled. He'd known Luke all his life. They'd played together as kids, drag-raced on the back roads and overindulged on beer on the banks of the Medina River. Now, since Luke had come home from the war in Iraq, they mostly argued over poker hands and commiserated about life's injustices. Brady took another drag from his glass. "I told you guys we should have gone to the steak house in New Braunfels. They serve a better grade of bourbon."

Jake smirked, lifted his drink and said, "I'd have much rather had the steak than these pitiful burgers. And face it, we're not leaving much of an impression at the Scoot 'n Boot tonight."

Brady returned the look and clinked his glass against Jake's. "Here's to the Not-so-Wild Bunch."

Luke checked his watch. "Can you believe it's only ten o'clock?"

"What?" Jake sank back in his chair. "I feel like I've been with you losers for hours."

Brady stared at him. "Losers, are we? What's that make you?"

Jake drained half his glass. "Point taken."

Luke reached for his wallet. "I'm in favor of calling it a night."

"At least we did one thing right tonight," Brady said. "Arranged to have one of the Cross Fox grooms be our designated driver."

Luke drank the last inch of liquid in his glass. "You know, we should have gone to my place and played poker. We could have come up with enough guys to make up a game."

"Not Cole though," Brady said, remembering the wild ride they'd taken at Christmas to bring Tessa and Cole together. Now they were inseparable. "And not Blake," Brady added.

Jake nodded, his expression far away, as if his thoughts were back at the Wild Card Saloon with Rachel and her baby. "Yeah," he said. "Love is definitely in the air in River Bluff."

"Which reminds me," Luke said. "My brother ran into Dobbs yesterday at the feed store. He said a sweet young thing showed up at Cross Fox a couple days ago. Something about a bet you made at a diner near

Blue Bonnet Farm." Luke's features displayed the cocky attitude he was known for. "Any truth to that?"

Brady's head filled with images of Molly. He pictured her blue eyes, her silky hair, the curves of her body in tight jeans. Her stubbornness. Her whiny kid. He tried to banish the thought. Brady loved Luke like a brother—most of the time—but he wasn't so sure he even liked him right now. He didn't want to be reminded of that ridiculous bet. "You'll meet her tomorrow at the hoedown."

Jake sat forward. "This sounds interesting. Tell me more, B.C."

Brady tossed a few bills on the table next to Luke's. "You'll have to wait. Now, drink up. Since we're not partying for real, I'm going to call our ride to come get us."

By consensus, fifteen minutes later the three members of the once notorious Wild Bunch piled into Marshall Carrick's Lincoln Town Car and headed toward each of their houses. At eleven o'clock, Brady found himself at the bottom step leading to the apartment over the tack room. And he was definitely feeling the effects of four cheap whiskeys.

MOLLY WIGGLED THE CORK out of the five-dollar bottle of chardonnay she'd bought at the convenience store earlier. She hardly ever drank, but she'd convinced herself she had ample motivation tonight. It had been a heck of a day and now she faced another in an endless string of Saturday nights in front of the

TV. She'd filled the glass halfway when she heard footsteps on the stairs. Setting down the drink, she quickly crossed to the bedroom, peeked inside at Sam sleeping in his cot and closed the door.

"Who can that be?" she said aloud, and then her question was answered when she recognized the familiar face in the front window. Looking flushed and half-frozen in the late night chill, Brady Carrick grinned through the glass at her.

"Open up," he hollered. "It's cold out here."

Annoyed, she shushed him with a finger to her lips, but walked to the door and pulled it open a few inches. "What?"

His grin stayed in place. "Let's play poker."

"Now?"

"Sure. Why not?"

"It's late. I've had a rough day." She caught the whiff of something tart and strong. "And you might be a bit drunk."

He hopped from one foot to the other, and she noticed he was wearing his leather jacket open, revealing a gray-and-white striped shirt tucked into a pair of black jeans. He'd obviously dressed for a night out. She wondered what had gone wrong.

He rested his forearm on the doorjamb. "I'm not drunk."

She raked her fingers through her hair. "You just want to play poker?"

"Yeah. Why else would I be here?"

She wasn't about to be tricked into answering

that leading question. But then she reminded herself that this was Brady Carrick, the man she was using to achieve her goals. She opened the door. "Okay, but when I say we're done, we're done."

"Fair enough." He came inside, tossed his jacket on a chair by the game table and sat on the sofa. Picking up the bottle of wine, he said, "Celebrating?"

She took the bottle from him. "Private party."

He leaned back, smiled. "Are you going to offer me a glass?"

"Wasn't planning on it."

"Okay. I would turn you down anyway. But you go ahead with yours."

Her nerves had suddenly started sending mysterious electric impulses to every part of her body, so what the heck? She picked up the glass and, still standing, took a sip.

Brady slid over on the sofa and patted the cushion next to him. "Make yourself comfortable."

She looked at the table. "I thought you wanted to play cards."

"I do. But we're talking tournament theory tonight. We can do that on the sofa." Molly sat, leaving a full cushion between them.

"Let's see how much you remember from before," he said. "In Texas Hold 'Em, how many cards is each player dealt?"

"Two."

"And what are the first three community cards called?"

"The flop."

"And the fourth community card?"

This was too easy. But she didn't tell him that she'd gone against his advice and made copious notes. "The turn card."

"And the fifth?"

"The river card."

He gave her a half grin. "I'm impressed."

"I've got a good memory."

"Most women do. Until now I've always found that something of a disadvantage in dealing with them."

She almost laughed thinking of all the women in Texas, and no doubt many other states, who'd "dealt" with Brady Carrick. "I can only imagine," she said.

"I'm not sure I want you to." He rested his arms on the back of the sofa. "I know you told me that you aren't married, but have you ever been?"

The question seemed to spring from nowhere and startled Molly out of the tentative comfort zone she'd begun to think could exist between her and Brady, at least when she'd had some wine to put her at ease. The subject of Kevin was definitely out-of-bounds, always would be until she chose to tell Brady that he once had a tragic connection to her husband. So, evading a direct answer, she said, "I do have a son sleeping a few feet away."

"I know. But come on, Molly, that's hardly proof that you were married."

She flinched and glared at him. "Yes, I was married."

"Oh. Mind me asking where the kid's father is?"

She certainly didn't intend to dredge up her private pain in front of the man who'd caused it. "I thought you came here to discuss theory."

He paused, staring at her. Finally he said, "Right. I did. There are four basic decisions with regard to betting in Texas Hold 'Em. Initially you can bet or not. After that you can either check, raise or fold. Now, considering that there are six to ten other players at the table who each have their two secret hole cards, let's figure out what you should do with, say, a king-jack combination." He studied her face. "Theoretically, and remembering the hierarchy of winning-hand combinations we discussed Thursday, what would you do?"

"I would probably bet," she said. "A king and jack are two strong cards."

"Okay. Right decision." He suggested three more test hands before he suddenly stopped talking cards. "Why won't you tell me about the kid's father?" he asked.

She answered with the biggest lie she'd ever told. "He doesn't concern you."

He pressed his hand on hers. "You know, you might be right."

"About what?"

"I could be a bit drunk."

She wiggled her hand free. "I think you're more than a bit drunk."

Brady edged closer to her. A haunting melody came from the television she'd left on in a useless attempt to ease the tension of his unexpected visit. Molly looked at the screen, saw the credits rolling at the end of the love story she'd been watching. "You're wrong," Brady said, his voice low and hoarse. "If I were more than a little drunk, I'd be kissing you right now."

His arm was on the back of the sofa. His fingertips touched her shoulder. "I wouldn't let you."

He smiled. "I'm sorry to hear that. I won't kiss you, then, but I'm going to think about kissing you. There's no harm in that."

She wasn't at all sure that was true, but she said, "I can't control what you think."

The music seemed to play forever, triumphant and sensual. She stared into Brady's face, unable to look away, no matter how hard she willed herself to. His eyes, wide and flecked with gold, were as warm and soothing as a spring breeze over her face. Her lips had gone dry and she trailed her tongue over them leaving a tingle on the moist flesh. He focused on her lips, parted his own and released a slow, undeniably seductive sigh. He reached up and, with one finger, tucked a strand of hair behind her ear.

The music finally stopped. An announcer previewed the next show. Molly was quite certain that she'd just experienced the hottest, sexiest kiss she'd ever gotten—and she only had her imagination to thank for it.

He stood. "I guess that's enough for tonight."

"Definitely."

He picked up his jacket, poured her another glass of wine and headed for the door. "See you tomorrow, Molly."

MOLLY'S GAZE remained fixed on the closed door for countless minutes. Finally, rousing herself from a sort of sublime stupor, she shut off the television and returned to the sofa.

Resentment and frustration warred within her. "Damn you, Brady Carrick."

She took a sip of wine, let its fruity tartness flow down her throat. When she set the glass on the table she crossed her arms in a desperate, unsatisfying embrace. She didn't want to feel anything for Brady but bitterness. She didn't want him to remind her of her loneliness and need.

She sat forward, braced her elbows on her knees and stared at the blank TV screen. Her life had been like that screen for so long, she'd begun to believe that emptiness would be all she would ever know. She'd even accepted that her father might be right. Whatever happened to her was her fault, because of her choices and failures.

And then the phantom man she'd hated for so long had caressed her with his eyes.

She grabbed a pillow from the sofa and held it to her chest. "What is wrong with you, Molly Jean?" she said. "You mean nothing more to Brady Carrick than a momentary diversion on a Saturday night." But Brady Carrick meant everything to her and she cautioned herself to remember why.

She stretched out on the couch, closed her eyes and once again heard the phone ring in that run-down house in Prairie Bend and her husband's voice telling her he was the new bull-riding champion of the Las Vegas Six Star Rodeo. Her heart had thrilled at his voice even after eight years of marriage.

"I won tonight, baby," he'd said. "Ten grand! I got a big, fat roll of cash right here in my pocket."

She'd begun to imagine paying off their car and credit-card debt. Maybe splurging on Sam. He'd given her an air kiss over the phone and said he'd see her the next day.

She'd gone to bed thinking her world was a wondrous place to be. Hopeful, happy, expectant. And then the phone rang again, two hours later, waking her from a deep, satisfying sleep.

"It's me again," Kevin had said. "You won't believe who I've run into. Brady Carrick. I've been talking to him in the bar at the Mirage."

Kevin had explained that the great Brady Carrick, former Dallas Cowboys star had been impressed with Kevin and his ten-grand prize. Molly had gotten out of bed and paced. Something about the bravado in Kevin's voice alarmed her. She'd told him to go back to his hotel and get some sleep.

He'd continued as if he hadn't heard her, claiming that Brady Carrick wasn't the god he'd once believed him to be. In fact, he'd said that Brady was really kind of an ass. And when Kevin said, "He thinks he knows everything about gambling," Molly got really worried. Her knees had gone weak. She'd asked Kevin if he'd been gambling or drinking.

She remembered his angry answer. "Shit, no, Mol. Give me a break."

She hadn't believed him. Kevin, the love of her life, could do stupid things when he'd been drinking.

He told her that Carrick had begged Kevin to play poker with him and some of his high-class buddies in a condo just off the strip.

"Kevin, are you crazy? You can't play with guys like that."

Kevin had insisted, saying that Brady was a loser with a bum knee and a fat lot of Vegas debt. "I can score big in this game," he'd said.

She'd pleaded with him not to risk that money in a poker game.

"I'm not risking it," he'd argued. "I'm *investing* it in a sure thing. Can't you believe in me for one night, Molly?"

And four hours later Molly received her third phone call from Las Vegas, this one from the police, informing her that her husband had jumped from the ninth floor of a Vegas condominium.

CHAPTER SEVEN

THE RUMBLE OF TRUCKS coming down the drive toward the main house woke Molly from a restless sleep. She got up, parted the window blinds and looked out at the gray dawn. Two cube vans, their side panels advertising the name of a party-supply store, pulled around the house and parked at the edge of the expansive backyard. The day before, the grass had been mowed and the holly shrubs and oak and pecan trees pruned. Wooden planters filled with geraniums ringed the manicured area where Marshall Carrick's birthday celebration would take place.

"What's going on, Mama?" Sam said from across the room. "Is it time to get up?"

She looked at the clock. 6:29 a.m. She'd promised to help Ruby and Serafina with final preparations this morning. A warm glow from the windows at the back of the big house proved that the kitchen was already bustling with activity. "It is for me, baby. But you can stay in bed a few more minutes if you want."

He sat up in his cot. "Isn't this the party day?"

"Yes, it is. I said I'd go to the big house to help, but I can get you up at the last minute."

He threw off the covers and headed for the bathroom. "I've got stuff to do."

She smiled, reached for her robe. "Well, then, okay. I'll fix your breakfast."

She had a glass of apple juice, toast and a bowl of cereal on the table when Sam came out a few minutes later wearing a hooded sweatshirt and corduroy pants. His socks were bunched around the tops of his sneakers, and the laces dragged on the floor. He sat down and began eating.

Carrying a mug of coffee, Molly headed to the bathroom. Ten minutes later, dressed in jeans and a pale yellow sweater, she came into the kitchen to refill her mug. Sam wasn't there. His bowl and plate were empty. Expecting to hear the television, she went into the living room. No Sam. But she shivered as a breeze swept in the open front door.

"Sam?" She went to the door and looked out on the small landing. She spotted him below near the horse statue in front of the stalls. He stood perfectly still in rapt attention, his eyes focused on the last stall where Molly could see a man moving inside.

When her eyes adjusted to the dawn, she recognized Brady's black felt hat as he crossed back and forth from one side of the stall to the other. Dust motes and bits of straw floated over the door, appearing like beads of gold in the slanting rays of the morning sun. She drew in a cleansing breath of fresh air and allowed herself to enjoy the peace of what she thought must be the rhythm of a new day on an awakening ranch.

Then she heard Brady's voice, the words indistinct but low and soothing as he opened the stall and led a reddish brown horse outside. Sam took a few steps toward him and called out, "Hey, Mr. Carrick."

Brady's head snapped around. The horse pranced back a couple of steps and Brady looped the lead rope around his fist.

Molly raced down the stairs. She didn't know much about horses beyond what she'd learned from Kevin, but she figured this chestnut beauty that had roused Brady from a warm bed was the thoroughbred at the center of the bet with his father and Dobbs. And she had enough horse sense of her own to realize the animal had been spooked by her son. She put her hands on Sam's shoulders and shushed him.

"I want to see the horse," Sam said. "I don't think I'll be scared of him."

Molly leaned over, spoke into his ear. "Not this horse, Sam. This is a thoroughbred. They can be very high-strung."

He looked up at her. "What's that mean?"

"It means they don't always take to strangers, and right now that's what you are to him." As an extra word of caution, she said, "You should always use good sense when you're around an animal you don't know. Just like you should tell me if you're going to leave the apartment. For now I want you to stay away from the horses."

Brady waved to them. "Does Sam want to see the colt?"

Molly shook her head. "No, it's okay—"

"Let him come."

"I don't think—"

Sam tugged on her shirtsleeve. "But, Mom..."

"Tie your shoes first, kid," Brady called. "And *walk* over here. Don't run."

Sam looked up at her. "Can I?"

She finally gave in. "Okay, but be careful."

He knelt on one knee and fumbled with the laces. When she bent to help him, he gave her a stern look. "Mr. Carrick said for me to do it."

She waited for Sam to accomplish what she could have done in one third the time. "Go slow," she reminded him. "Don't startle the horse."

She chewed on a fingernail as she watched Sam approach. Brady stopped him before he came too close. He leaned over and spoke. Occasionally Sam nodded. Then, with Brady walking between Sam and the horse, they headed around the end of the stable to a fenced-in pasture a few hundred feet away.

Molly took a normal breath.

"Boys and their horses," someone said behind her. "Here in Texas it's as natural as bluebonnets on the hillsides."

Molly turned to face Angela Carrick. This morning Angela's hair was neatly pulled into a barrette at her nape and she wore tan twill pants and a brown leather jacket. Her eyes were clear. Much different from the only other time Molly had seen her.

"You look worried," Angela said. "Don't be."

"My son has always been fascinated with horses, but he's never had any experience with one."

"Brady will watch him. Despite what you may have learned about Carrick men, responsibility isn't one of their failings."

"I beg your pardon?"

"You must know my son very well. Otherwise you wouldn't be here." Angela paused, waiting for Molly to respond. When Molly kept silent, she continued. "Naturally I assumed that you and Brady… It's perfectly fine with me."

"You assumed wrong, Mrs. Carrick," Molly snapped. "Your son and I have a business relationship. Nothing more."

"Oh? Well, then, my mistake. I must admit that I'm often kept out of the loop where the men of this household are concerned." She sat down on a bench at the base of the stairs, leaving room for Molly. "Why don't we wait for your son here?"

Molly watched Brady open a gate to the pasture and lead the horse inside the fence. Sam stayed outside, hanging over a rail. "I think I'd rather stand, Mrs. Carrick."

"Call me Angela. I feel old enough already."

Keeping her eyes on Sam, Molly said, "What did you mean a minute ago when you said, 'despite what

I may have learned'? Is there something I should know about Brady?"

"I didn't mean to alarm you. Brady is a fine man. So is his father. As honorable as the day is long. In fact, if they have a fault in common, it's that their sense of honor is almost too pervasive."

Honorable? Brady was just the opposite. But at least he hadn't forced his traveling money on her or turned her away from Cross Fox.

Angela sipped from her tall mug. "Marshall can be difficult to live with," she said, following the comment with a forced smile. "Of course, I suppose he would say that I'm no picnic, either."

Having no idea how to respond to such an intimate disclosure, Molly looked at the sky. "This is a big day for your family. I think the weather will cooperate."

"Yes, it's a nice start for the annual midwinter hoedown. I don't see too many of them—mornings, I mean. But this event means a lot to Marshall, so I rose to the challenge." Her lips hinted at another smile. "So to speak."

Brady moved to the gate, the lead rope and halter dangling from his hand. The pretty chestnut horse galloped around the open field. "Is that the horse your son just bought in Prairie Bend?" Molly asked Angela.

"Oh, honey, I wouldn't know. I can't tell one horse from another. It probably is, though. Brady's all excited about that animal and when he's got something on his mind he can't sleep. I'm not surprised to see him out here so early. Amber Mac is the horse's name, if I recall Brady telling me right."

"That's appropriate," Molly said. "His coat almost seems amber in the sunlight."

Angela looked over her shoulder. The men in the trucks had unloaded their gear. Some of them spread canvas awnings across the lawn while others snapped folding chairs open. "I should get back," she said. "I'm supposed to tell the men what goes where, that sort of thing." She shrugged a shoulder. "Though we've used the same party company for years and everything's always been put up the same way."

She stood. "That's another thing about Carrick men. They worship tradition. They like knowing that some things never change. I suppose that's why they're both into bloodlines and training horses. You buy right and you do the best you can with your product and success should be guaranteed. Unfortunately that philosophy doesn't always extend to the people in their lives." She sighed. "People can let you down."

She was heading toward the house when she abruptly stopped and turned back to Molly. "You're coming to the party, aren't you?"

"I'll help in the kitchen."

"Nonsense. We've hired dozens of people to help. You're every bit a guest here. And you're Brady's guest. That alone makes it imperative that you attend." After another moment she said, "Do you have anything to wear?"

Molly looked down at her jeans and sweater. "I could maybe find something a bit fancier than this."

Angela smiled, for real this time. "This is a Texas party, honey. You've got to have embroidery and leather and lots of fringe hanging in all the right places."

Molly laughed. "Then I guess I don't."

"I'll send something over. Serafina's girls left several outfits here when they moved up to Austin. I'm sure one of them will fit you."

"Thanks, Angela. Would you tell Ruby and Serafina I'll be over in a few minutes?"

"Will do," Angela called over her shoulder. After a moment Molly became aware of footsteps pounding behind her. Turning, she found herself staring into Sam's smiling face. "Did you see me, Mom?"

"I sure did."

"Amber Mac is really neat, isn't he?"

"I didn't get such a close look, but I'll take your word for it." The irony of this conversation suddenly struck her. Kevin, had been an accomplished rodeo rider, and yet, today, for the first time—and with a man who was practically a stranger—Sam had walked side by side with one of the animals he'd fantasized about for years.

Sam stuck his hand in hers. "I think Mac likes me, Mom."

"I'm sure he does. What's not to like about my Sammy?"

When they reached the steps, she felt a larger, stronger hand brush her shoulder.

"Good morning." Brady smiled, a mischievous expression in his green eyes. "I'm still thinking about the kiss," he whispered.

She didn't have a chance to respond. He touched the brim of his hat. "See you at the party," he said, and followed his mother toward the house.

A WHOLE PIG went on the spit at 8:00 a.m. By nine, tables and chairs for two hundred sat under three tents on the lawn. By ten, a wooden dance floor was in place next to the hastily built bandstand. By noon the boys from the Lonesome Coyote Band were tuning their instruments and doing sound checks. A half hour later, the musicians ordered their first beers from the bartender who wore a three-quarter length oilskin duster and Navajo red-stitched black boots that screamed, your-feet-will-be-killing-you-by-the-time-the-sun-goes-down.

At one o'clock the first guests began to arrive, and Brady watched the Cross Fox yard become a living, vibrant tribute to all segments of the south-central Texas population, from wranglers to politicians. He welcomed Hub Parker, Becky's father, and spoke to Wade Barstow, the man who owned nearly half the buildings on Main Street.

Blake and Annie Smith arrived next. Though several years in age and experience separated Brady and Blake, the friendship between the two had grown since Cole Lawry first introduced Blake to the weekly poker games. Annie, Cole's sister and Blake's wife—for a second time—gave her husband a quick kiss and went to join friends. That was just like Annie. She was probably already taking notes for a human-interest story about the hoedown. She wouldn't have any trouble getting folks to open up to her. Everyone in town loved to give their opinions to Annie.

Brady was pleased for Blake and Annie. After what his friend had been through, being locked up in a foreign prison, coming home to find the life and the woman he'd left behind had changed… But the old Blake was now back, and he and Annie were having a baby and building a future together.

Blake came up to Brady and put his arm around his shoulders. "How's it going, buddy?" he said. "The old man treating you okay?"

Thank goodness Brady could answer truthfully. "We're getting along pretty well, actually."

"I hope that new thoroughbred is working out for you," Blake added. "I think everyone in the county knows that Macintosh Red's colt has taken up residence at Cross Fox."

"And I have you and Colin Warner to thank for that," Brady said. "Your assistant was sure right about this horse. Amber Mac and I are going to see a lot of winner's circles if everything goes the way I want it to."

"I'm just glad to see you've got such a positive outlook, considering how you left Vegas." Blake frowned. "I wish I'd been here to help you through that."

Brady often wondered if things might have been

different if he'd had Blake to talk to after that fateful poker game. Blake was older than the rest of the Wild Bunch, saner, always the voice of reason. He might have been able talk Brady through one of the lowest points in his life. And Blake would have done it if he could have. He would have been there when Brady needed him.

"I've put it behind me," Brady said, though it was mostly a lie.

"I hope you buried the guilt with it because you can't take other people's faults on yourself. It'll cut you down faster than the meanest rattlesnake on the prairie." He glanced around the yard. "Now, where's that lucky lady I've been hearing about? The one in the most talked about wager in River Bluff history?"

"Damn, Blake, you mean, word's out in town about that stupid bet?"

"Annie tells me it's big news." Blake laughed and pointed over Brady's shoulder. "And I also heard about it from those two gossips."

Brady watched Jake and Luke saunter up.

"Yeah, where is she?" Jake asked. "Rachel and I only came to this shindig for one reason."

"Hell, you came to load up on Ruby's spareribs and Serafina's guacamole," Brady said.

Jake grinned. "Oh, right. Three reasons. So now, while Rachel is off acquainting half of River Bluff with the baby, I want to see the future poker phenom."

At that moment Molly came out of the kitchen carrying a huge tray of nachos and salsa. Brady would have offered to help her, but he would have been too late. One of the Cross Fox grooms, practically tripping over his feet, had already relieved her of the burden.

Brady couldn't blame the guy for playing Galahad. Molly looked fantastic in a black gaucho skirt with a decoration of purple sage on the hem. On top, she wore a long-sleeved plum jacket with silver studs plunging to a single button at her waist. Brady's gaze dropped immediately to the deep V of the jacket. He was relieved *and* disappointed to see a thin strip of pink fabric covering her cleavage. Resting against her breastbone was the smoky turquoise charm necklace. Her dark hair, held back from her face with a simple silver clip, curled at her shoulders.

Luke whistled. "Hell, Brady, she doesn't need to learn poker. Just sit her at the table and watch the other players make fools of themselves."

Brady's next words were a reflection of his reaction to this new and unexpected version of Molly. "Be careful what you say. She's a mother. Got a seven-year-old kid."

"Hasn't hurt her any in my opinion," Luke said. "Introduce me so I can get her to promise me a dance later."

"I don't know about that dance," Brady said, feeling oddly territorial. "All these people here today might overwhelm her. She'll probably only dance with me." That was a ridiculously possessive statement, and Brady avoided looking at his friends.

Molly wasn't shy and she'd darned well decide for herself who she'd dance with. She smiled at his friends and shook their hands.

"So I hear you're headed for Vegas and the quarterly tournament finals," Jake said.

"I'm going to try," said Molly.

Jake slanted a look at Brady. "If this guy gives you any trouble, just let me or Luke know. We play poker with a bunch of guys on Wednesday nights and I'm sure we could find you another teacher if Mr. Dark Side here gets to be too much to handle."

"Brady has a dark side?" she asked.

"He can brood with the best of them," Luke answered.

"Cut it out," Brady said, scowling. "If I have a dark side, it's because I've known you idiots for too many years."

Luke grinned. "Don't mind us, Molly. Truth is, our pal here is finally coming around. He's starting to act like the Brady of old. And we kind of like him that way."

"I don't know him well enough to say if that's a good thing or not. I just hope he knows poker."

Luke looked at Jake. Both men shrugged. "He knows poker," Jake said. "And a little about football. And hopefully something about racehorses. Otherwise that bet he made with his father and Dobbs won't amount to a hill of beans even if you succeed in the casino."

"Hey, he doesn't have to worry about Amber Mac," Blake pointed out.

"That's right," Brady said. "Mac comes highly recommended." He shouldered Luke into Jake. "Aren't there some other women around here you guys want to annoy? I've had about all the morale building I can take for one day."

"And I've got some bean dip to bring from the kitchen," Molly said.

The group broke up. Blake joined Annie. Jake and Luke headed toward the bar. Brady held the back door for Molly as she walked ahead of him into the mudroom and immediately bumped into Sam. The kid, with a giant-sized brownie in one pudgy hand and a ginger cookie shaped like a cowboy in the other, was running for the exit.

"Whoa," Brady said, grabbing the boy by his arm. "Obviously Serafina didn't see you charging through the kitchen like a wild mustang, or you wouldn't have these goodies."

Sam licked his finger. "Ruby gave them to me. I guess she doesn't care about the charging part."

"Sorry about that," Brady said to Molly.

She smiled. "What are you sorry about?"

"The brownie. The food's being carried to the tents right now. And unless this kid knows a secret lunch fairy, then I figure he's doing things in reverse." When she didn't respond, he added, "Dessert first?"

She waved off his comment. "Oh. That's okay. Normally I make sure he's had a good lunch, but today's special. It's a party." She opened the door for Sam. "Go on, sweetie. I saw some kids about your age outside."

He headed through the door. "I'm playing with Dodger."

Once Sam was out of hearing range, Brady leaned against the entrance to the kitchen and looked at Molly.

"You have something else you want to say?" she asked.

"Maybe it's none of my business, but do you think that's wise?"

"What?"

"Letting him eat all that sugar now?"

She darted past him into the kitchen. "You're right. It's none of your business."

He followed her, lowering his voice so he wouldn't be heard by the help hired to keep two hundred people fed and happy. "Look, I don't mean to cut into your territory, but it seems to me poor eating habits could be the reason..."

Her eyes practically spit fire. "Don't say it."

He knew he was on shaky ground, but what the heck. He'd obviously broached a forbidden topic and wasn't going to back down now. She had to know her kid was shy and backward and afraid of his own shadow. Even Brady, who didn't know much about kids, could tell Sam needed a good dose of self-confidence. He reached out to touch her arm. She jerked it away. "Molly, anybody can see that Sam is...overweight."

"It's baby fat," she said. "He'll lose it."

"He's not a baby."

Her back grew as rigid as Marshall's flagpole in

the backyard. "You have no right to criticize how I raise him. You have no idea what he's been through."

"True, but I just thought, while you're here, this might be the perfect environment for him to change some of his…"

Her eyes narrowed to slits. "That's enough, Brady. You don't know a thing about my son."

She stormed out of the room and Brady was left wondering how he'd managed to make such an ass of himself when he was trying to help. Plus, how was he going to convince her to make time for poker later on?

ONCE SHE LEFT THE KITCHEN, Molly had no idea where she was going. The house was huge and she was a stranger in it, a stranger who didn't have clearance to wander its many rooms looking for a place to vent her anger.

She headed down a long hallway, past what she assumed was a powder room since a line of people had accumulated outside the door. Eventually light drew her to the end of the hall where the afternoon sun speared through open double doors onto a polished mahogany floor. She looked into a glassed-in six-sided haven filled with wicker furniture and lush hanging baskets. She'd noticed this room from the outside of the house the day she'd arrived and its quaint shape had captured her imagination then.

She crossed the threshold and strode to a window with a view of the side yard. Under normal circumstances she would have had a hard time staying angry in such a sun-washed, welcoming hideaway, but not today. The head of steam she'd worked up with Brady wasn't going to dissipate very soon.

How dare Brady Carrick presume to tell her anything about her son? He didn't know one detail about Sam's life—not even that it was Brady, himself, who'd changed it so drastically. He hadn't watched her and Sam grieve. He hadn't seen her son battle a sense of inferiority that worsened after they moved in with his overly critical grandfather. He hadn't seen Sam's gratitude over every dollar-store toy he'd gotten at Christmas. And he hadn't watched Sam struggle to be normal without a father.

"So what if he's a little overweight?" Molly said. She wasn't going to deny him the one thing that seemed to make him happy. He found comfort in food, and she found comfort in giving it to him. Maybe that was wrong, but at this point in Sam's life, Molly didn't care.

She leaned on the windowsill, looked across at the stables and watched her son play with Dodger. This morning he'd been so excited with the old straw cowboy hat and vest Dobbs had brought him from a trunk left by one of the Cross Fox employees. And now, while other children had their faces painted and watched a magician perform sleight-of-hand wonders, Sam rolled on the ground with that dog, away from the crowd, away from the party he couldn't wait to attend a few hours ago.

She squinted, keeping the tears in her eyes from spilling over. "Sammy, I'm so sorry," she whispered. "There hasn't been any magic in your life for so long."

"I love that crazy little dog."

Molly drew in a quick breath and turned away from the window.

"Sorry," Angela said. "I seem to be sneaking up on you a lot today. I don't mean to."

"No. It's fine. I probably shouldn't be in here."

"Of course you can be here. What's this room for if not as a respite from the men in this house, though sometimes they are guilty of sneaking in, too."

Molly noticed the nearly empty wineglass in Angela's hand. The woman set it down on a table and fiddled with the suede fringe hanging from the sleeve of her cream-colored jacket studded with marcasite and pink quartz. The jacket and matching skirt probably cost more than Molly's entire wardrobe. And the teal snakeskin boots on Angela's dainty feet would have set Molly back six months' wages. Realizing she was staring, Molly returned to the window. "So Dodger is yours?"

"I suppose mostly, though Marshall brought him home three years ago. But I coddle him when the men never do. I guess that's why Dodger doesn't know his place around here." She sighed. "Can you imagine? A dog with an identity crisis." She stared blankly out the window. "I guess that's why I'm so connected to him," she said. "He kind of reminds me of… Well, never mind."

And Dodger is a lot like my Sam, too, Molly thought.

"I believe that silly dog knows that sometimes it's easier to stay on the fringe of the men's lives," Angela said. She picked up her glass, drained the last of the wine and held it up. "I'm ready for another. Care to join me?"

Molly shook her head. "No, thanks. I'm going to stay here, if that's all right, and watch Sam."

"Suit yourself." Angela walked to the door but stopped before going out. "Hello, darling. Tired of partying?"

Brady stepped through the doorway. "No. I just heard Molly's voice and I was looking for her."

"How lucky, then, that you found her." With a small wave, Angela headed down the hall.

Molly resumed looking out the window. She heard Brady's footsteps as he came closer but didn't acknowledge his presence.

"I'm sorry," he said. "You're right. I was out of line."

"Yes, you were."

"Don't let what I said ruin the party for you. There are some really great people here, as well as boot-kickin' country music. The dancing should start any minute and I thought you and I might—"

She held up her hand. "If you're about to suggest that we dance, I have to tell you I'm not really in the mood."

"Heck, everybody's in the mood for dancing at a Texas hoedown." He paused and started to smile. "Those folks who know how to dance, that is."

When she didn't respond, he grinned. "That's it, isn't it? You don't know how to dance."

"I never said that."

He didn't let the subject drop. "Good grief, woman, do I have to teach you everything?"

She didn't want to smile. She was still mad at him for interfering with Sam. "Let's keep it to poker, okay?"

"Fair enough. For now." He watched out the window a minute. "The kid really likes that dog."

"Yes, he does."

"The partying ends around sundown. How about a lesson later?"

It's easier to stay on the fringe of the men's lives. She wondered what in Angela's background had made her say that. True or not, Molly wasn't about to stay away from Brady. Not now. She was determined to grab every bit of knowledge from him she could. "Sure. I've got to get Sam ready for his first day of school tomorrow, but any time after eight should be okay."

"Fine. I'll see you then."

"Sober?"

He smiled. "Plan to be."

"Okay."

He left, and Molly kept her vigil. Sam was rolling in the grass, the dog scrambling all over him. To someone who didn't know better, he looked like a normal kid playing with his dog in one of the most idyllic settings Molly had ever seen. But appearances were deceiving. For months after Kevin died, every time she smiled at a customer, Molly knew that was true. And maybe it was true for Brady. Despite all this opulence, all the breaks he seemed to have going for him, his friends claimed he had a dark side. Why? What prompted Brady to brood?

If she won in Vegas, Molly would look forward to revealing the truth to him about who she was and that she'd used the skills he'd taught her to reclaim the life he'd stolen from her. She'd look into his eyes and tell him she was Molly Davis, the wife of the cowboy he'd stripped of his dignity. She'd watch his face change. Maybe then she'd finally discover if Brady Carrick had a conscience.

CHAPTER EIGHT

EARLY MONDAY MORNING Molly and Sam left the ranch and drove into town where she picked up the highway that would take them to the elementary school. Sam was in the passenger seat, his backpack between his feet and his nylon lunch bag in his lap.
"So, how are you feeling?" Molly asked him.

"Okay."

"Aren't you glad you met some kids at the party yesterday who'll be in your grade?"

"Guess so."

"That one boy was really nice. What was his name?"

"Jerry?"

"Right. You liked him, didn't you?"

"He was okay. He played with Dodger, too, and that was cool."

"Maybe he can come over sometime and play with you and Dodger again."

Sam shrugged. "Yeah, maybe."

Molly turned into the parking lot. Sam appeared to be doing fine. He'd always liked school and she hoped his experience in River Bluff wouldn't be any different. If he was happy here and if she won enough money in the tournament, she almost wanted to stay here to open her shop. The town was pleasant and maybe she would make friends, too.

In fact, she saw Becky Howard, the nurse from the clinic, walking toward the building. Molly rolled down her window and called to her.

"Hi there," Becky said. She leaned over and looked in the car. "How's our cowboy doing?"

"I'm good," Sam said. "My knee doesn't even hurt."

"Do you have a child in school?" Molly asked.

"Yes, but he's in the high school over there." She pointed to a large building in the same complex. "I'm just checking on first-aid supplies."

"Don't tell me," Molly said. "You're the school nurse, as well as the one who runs the clinic?"

"You got it. My office is in the high school, but I'm available if they need me for all three facilities."

Molly looked at Sam. "That's good to know, isn't it, Sam? Mrs. Howard is here."

He nodded.

Becky pointed to an empty parking space. "Better grab that if you're coming in. About ten minutes from now this place will be crazy. River Bluff only has about nine hundred people, but we have two and half times that number of students here. We're one of the educational centers for the county."

Molly drove into the spot and waited for Sam to get his gear. They walked with Becky into the building, and she pointed them to the office.

A pleasant-looking middle-aged woman at the counter asked, "Can I help you?" Her name tag identified her as Fran Wardell.

Molly explained that she wanted to enroll her son and the woman got the appropriate paperwork from under the counter and slid it across to her. She pulled a pen from a cup shaped like an apple basket and handed it to Molly. "So, you new in town?" she asked.

Molly said she was and started filling in the blanks. The woman leaned across the counter and read her address upside down. "It says here you're livin' out at Cross Fox."

Molly continued inputting Sam's information. "Yes. Temporarily."

The woman twisted a pencil threaded through her curly red hair. "I know who you are. You're that woman everybody's talking about, the one in the poker-tournament wager."

Molly stopped writing and stared at the woman. She tried to place her as a guest at the party yesterday, but she didn't look familiar. "Word gets around in this town."

"You're not kidding. I didn't make it out to the hoedown, but I still heard about all the goings-on."

Molly finished and pushed the papers back toward Fran. "You know Brady well?" she asked.

"Oh, sure. I've known him since he was enrolled in this school." Fran smiled at Sam. "Second grade, huh?"

He nodded.

"You're lucky. Your teacher's gonna be Miss

Harmon. She had a kid move away at Christmas so you'll take his spot. You'll like her. All the kids do."

Molly expected the woman to come around the counter and escort Sam to class, but she seemed more interested in pumping Molly for information. "So, I hear you're not married," she said.

"No."

Fran lowered her voice. "I'm single myself. You'll find in River Bluff the men are a breed to themselves. I've dated a few of them." She turned to a younger woman who was filing manila folders. "Karen, tell—" she ran her finger under Molly's name on the paperwork "—Molly here what we say about the men in this town."

The younger woman laughed. "It's nice to step out with a real cowboy, only it'd be better if we didn't have to give them a flea dip before the date."

Fran grinned. "That's what we say. You've also got to accept that half the men in this town are here to hide from something."

Brady? Molly could understand if he'd come home to hide from what he'd done in Vegas.

Fran laughed. "I see the wheels turning in your head, honey. You don't have to worry about Brady. His mama doesn't allow any fleas in her house. And I hear he's tamed down since his younger days." She finally walked around to Sam. "You ready to see your classroom?"

"Sure."

Molly gave him a quick kiss, explained that she'd

be back in the afternoon when school let out and told him to have a great day. Before Fran and Sam headed down the hall, the secretary said, “Come into town some night, Molly. You’ll usually find a bunch of us at the Scoot ’n Boot Saloon putting back a couple of cold ones. Us girls can give you some pointers on poker, too.”

Molly waved halfheartedly. “Thanks.” She left and got in her car. Today was a first for her, as well as for Sam. As soon as she got back to the ranch she was going to try to make sense out of that drawer full of receipts. But she’d have to stop thinking about one particular man and why he’d probably come back to River Bluff to hide.

MOLLY PUSHED her reading glasses back onto the bridge of her nose and blew her bangs off her forehead with a frustrated breath. When she’d come in from taking Sam to school, she’d decided to start her new job by tackling Cross Fox’s petty-cash receipts. Finding the kitchen quiet and sunny, she’d sat at the table with a metal box full of slips of paper. Now, at 9:30 a.m., after a half hour of work, she wondered how anyone had been able to make sense of the Carrick family’s records.

She spread receipts in front of her and began sorting them into piles, one each for household expenses, travel, stable upkeep and miscellaneous. The miscellaneous records were already threatening to fall off the edge of the table.

She was so engrossed in her efforts to pigeonhole the Carricks' spending into some semblance of order she didn't hear anyone enter the room.

"Suited connectors," Brady said.

She clapped her hand on her heart and looked over her shoulder. "You scared me."

"Sorry. Suited connectors."

"Two running hole cards of the same suit, like a six and seven of hearts."

"Right. Big slick."

She tried not to think about the way he filled out his tailored buff-colored sports jacket, boot-cut jeans and soft beige shirt. "Any ace-king combination." She turned back to her work. "Now, go away."

"I can't." He set his hat on the table, pulled out a chair and sat on it backward. "This is a pop quiz after last night's lesson."

He'd presented her with a glossary of Texas Hold 'Em terms the night before. She'd found the new vocabulary interesting and colorful and when Brady left, she'd felt more connected to the game that might ultimately change her future. Tapping her pencil on the tabletop, she looked at him. "If I get an A, will you leave me alone?"

"Probably. But not because you got a good grade. I have to leave for San Antonio in a few minutes. I have meetings the next couple of days at the racetrack."

"So that's why you're decked out like it's Saturday night."

He smiled. "Gotta keep up appearances. Heads up."

"When only two players are left in the hand and they're competing with each other one-on-one."

"Okay, what about—"

"Stop." Molly picked up a scrap of paper. "I've got one for you."

"Shoot."

"Cowgirl Corral."

"A really cool tavern in San Antonio near the racetrack."

Molly had to assume he was right. "Now, what am I supposed to do with this hundred-and-twenty dollar bar tab in the petty-cash box?"

"File it under Brady's entertainment budget."

She smirked. "I'll bet."

"No, really. That's what it is. What's the date?"

She read the fine print. "September 10."

"That's during Retama Park's thoroughbred season. We won a big stakes race that day and I took the director of racing and a few of the trainers out for a celebration."

"This seems like more than a simple celebration. Especially when it includes dancing cowgirls."

He grinned. "I didn't think you'd ever been there."

"I guessed."

"I'll take you sometime, prove to you that it's a legitimate tax deduction—and that the dancers are fully clothed in these cute little—"

"Spare me the details." She waved another receipt at him. "How about this one? Red Bull."

"What?"

"A case of it purchased at the 7-Eleven on September 28th."

He scratched his head. "Isn't it my turn?"

She sighed. "I suppose. Go ahead."

"Mucking."

"Stalls or poker hands?"

He smiled. "What do you think?"

"Mucking is the same thing as folding a hand. I told you before. I have a good memory."

"So do I. Let's see. You asked me about the Red Bull on September 28th. I was driving to Arizona to deliver a pair of four-year-olds to a rancher in Sedona. Dobbs and I left at six Thursday morning after playing poker the night before. You'll find gasoline receipts and a drive-through bill from Wendy's, as well as the drink purchase. Those items are all legitimate costs of doing business. You wouldn't have wanted me to doze off behind the wheel."

"No. I'm just glad I don't have to go through years of these receipts. I'll bet they all have a story."

"My stories only go back a year and a half," he said. "I lived somewhere else before that."

Right. You were living where you could take advantage of poor rodeo cowboys like Kevin. Even though she knew the answer to her next question, she asked anyway. "So, where were you?"

"Las Vegas." He stood and picked up his hat. "The lost years."

She dropped the Red Bull receipt onto the travel expense pile. "You were lost?"

"Yeah, like a lot of people who call Las Vegas home." He pulled his hat low on his brow. "I gotta go."

"I heard your friends talking yesterday. You have poker at Jake's place Wednesday night?"

"Sure do. And I'll be late tonight and tomorrow. So you're off the hook for another lesson." He headed toward the back door. "You and Sam can both do homework."

Molly repositioned her glasses and picked up another receipt. "I may have better things to do."

His boots scraped on the kitchen floor as he stopped, turned around. "Yeah? Like what?"

She carefully recorded a number in a column on the ledger pad. "I've made some friends in town. I might just join them at the Scoot 'n Boot one of these nights."

Heat flooded Molly's face. Why had she said that? She'd never go to the Scoot 'n Boot. She wouldn't leave Sam. And she wouldn't fit in a place like that anyway. So why did she say it?

He stood behind her. She heard his breathing. After a moment he said, "A word of advice, Molly."

She couldn't look at him. "Hmm?"

"The cowboys at the Scoot 'n Boot…the same guys hang out there every night and most of the women in town know to steer clear of them. It's a case of same butts, different bar stools. So if you're looking for a meaningful relationship—"

"I'm not."

"Then by all means, go. Try dancing with those boys and see where it gets you."

He left, and Molly blew out the breath she'd been holding. She tried to concentrate on her work, but the numbers swam in front of her eyes. Meaningful relationship? Fat chance.

BRADY HAD A BAD COUPLE OF DAYS. He couldn't get the image of Molly at the Scoot 'n Boot out of his mind. Molly and those roustabout cowboys hanging around her, asking her to dance. Would she do the two-step with them when she wouldn't with him? Still, he tried to keep his mind on business. He and a few dozen other trainers from around the San Antonio area met with Harry Caufield, the director of racing at San Antonio's Retama Park. They discussed availability of stalls at the track and the upcoming racing schedule, each contributing details about stakes and claiming races and which horses they hoped to enter.

The meetings had been typical get-togethers, Texan horseman-style. Harry picked up the tabs in the exclusive Turf and Field Club, the glass-enclosed trackside members-only restaurant. Everybody dressed up, talked too loud, drank too much and pretended to like cigars. Brady, representing Cross Fox Ranch, got the concessions he wanted and scored points with Harry, the one man at Retama who could make or break a horse's career by the placement he gave him in races. But Brady's heart hadn't been in it. His conversation with Molly had left him thinking—too much.

Now, Wednesday night, dressed in comfortable clothes, he sped along the two-lane road that ran alongside the Medina River on his way to the Wild Card Saloon. And he was still thinking about Molly. His father and Dobbs were in the car behind him. They'd both agreed to play tonight but brought their own vehicle. That wasn't unusual for the older guys. They often left after the first two tournaments—usually claiming fatigue, but almost always light in the pockets.

Brady still couldn't figure out why he'd felt compelled to answer Molly about Vegas. He didn't enjoy thinking about that time—his messy divorce, his freewheeling spending habits while he was married and careless betting decisions afterward. These were decisions he wished he could make over again.

He looked in his rearview mirror. His dad was still tailing him along the winding river road. Brady concentrated on his driving. It wouldn't do for him to get lost in thought in the dark and make a driving mistake. They still had a good five miles to go before reaching the Wild Card.

But his thoughts wouldn't leave him alone and he found himself once again sitting at that bar in the Mirage on what had started out as a normal night. He would have won a few poker hands, lost a few and gone home to sleep it off. If only that rodeo cowboy hadn't come into the bar and settled himself at the very next stool.

The guy—slim, wiry, with a leathery neck and

face—had set down a beer and said, "Damn. Aren't you Brady Carrick?"

That was a reaction Brady got a lot a few years ago. He'd answered as he always did. "I used to be."

The cowboy extended a long lean arm across the top of the bar, introduced himself and said he was in town for the rodeo. Then he admitted to being a fan of Brady's since his Longhorn College days.

When the cowboy said he'd won the big prize in bull riding, Brady offered to buy him a beer.

Kevin had raised his bottle and said, "I'll surely let you. This is only my first one, but I might be inclined to do some celebrating tonight."

They'd talked for about an hour before Les Borne, one of Brady's poker friends, met up with him. Brady stood and wished the cowboy luck.

Kevin had grabbed him by his arm. His eyes had shone with an inner fire Brady had seen much too often in Vegas, and he said the words Brady later wished he'd never heard. "Don't suppose you might have an open seat."

"No, sorry," Brady had said immediately.

"Yes, we do," Les had said turning to Kevin. "You know how to play?"

Brady stared at the blacktop rushing under his tires. The Wild Card sat just ahead. He slowed, put on his blinker. This night of poker would be nothing like that one. The stakes weren't nearly so high.

CHAPTER NINE

BRADY GOT OUT of his truck and waited for his dad and Dobbs. Marshall stepped from the town car, stood with his hands on his hips and scrutinized the Wild Card from its new roof to the fresh coat of paint on its siding. "This place is actually looking better," he said.

Brady smiled at him. "Not bad for a historic landmark. It still needs work inside though."

Marshall chuckled. "The hell? This place is no historic landmark. I don't know of any old roadhouses that are."

"Maybe not in the literal sense. But it's historic to the guys who used to play poker here on a regular basis, you included, I might add."

Marshall looked at Dobbs. "We could be setting up in the office at the Cross Fox stables about now, if we'd stuck to our guns and hadn't let Brady talk us into coming here. In a few minutes Serafina would be bringing in platters of hot tacos and fajitas."

"You might as well get over it," Dobbs said in a tone devoid of sympathy. "Poker's poker, and I don't much care what the food is. I'm here to play."

Brady headed to the door. "And there's nothing wrong with pizza."

Marshall rubbed his stomach with the dramatic flair of someone anticipating heartburn and followed Brady. "Hope somebody remembered the poker chips."

The revered silver box that held all their card-playing paraphernalia had passed through many hands over the years, and everyone who'd been responsible for its safekeeping had taken his job seriously. "Jake's got them."

He held the door and they went inside, stopping in the area that used to be the bar just ahead of a small apartment in back where Jake had been living since he came back to River Bluff. Rachel and her baby had occupied the upstairs apartment for a while, but she and Jake had progressed to living as a family in the downstairs apartment now. The room was filled at this moment with the usual suspects, minus one. There was Blake, the nervous dad-to-be, with his cell phone in his hand in case Annie called; Jake with the poker case in front of him on the table; Luke, his hat at a cocky angle over his thick hair, now grown out from the military cut; and Cole, joking because life with Tessa was good. Luke, Cole and Jake—they all still looked a lot like the hell-bent-for-trouble teenagers they used to be.

Harold Knutson from the hardware store was also seated, a likeable enough guy whose wife, Sally, was the local beautician. And Ed Falconetti, owner of

The Longhorn Café and River Bluff's transplant from New Jersey. He still had his rough-edged accent but after years in town, he fit in almost like a native.

"Only nine guys tonight?" Brady said, choosing a seat at the oblong table. "Where's Hap?"

"Couldn't make it," Luke said of the trusted employee at the Chisum family ranch. "It was too late to get a replacement."

Cole grinned. "Yeah. I wanted to call you to bring Molly. I'd finally get to meet her, and it'd be good experience for her to play with sharps like us."

Brady smirked. "Right. I'm trying to encourage her, not turn her off cards forever."

Harold Knutson cleared his throat. "I wouldn't let Cole call you. I don't like women in the game."

Luke rolled his eyes. "Oh, you'd like Molly— Hey, Brady, what happened to her at the hoedown? I was going to ask her to dance."

Brady shrugged his pretended indifference. "I don't think she knows how to dance."

Luke's eyebrows shot up. "No kidding? Well, here's your chance, buddy. Wrap your arms around that pretty little thing and teach her. It's your responsibility as a Texan, not to mention a helluva good opportunity to get close to her."

As if Brady hadn't already pondered the advantages of instructing Molly in the two-step. He glared at Luke. "We're here to play cards, Chisum, not to map out a strategy for me to get a woman."

Luke raised his hands in a defensive gesture.

"Hell, that's fine with me. If you don't want to teach her, I'll volunteer."

"Enough talk about women," Harold said. "Deal the cards."

Luke grabbed a chair. "Have you ever tried being anything other than an old fart, Knut?"

The man gave him a wry smile. "Nope. And I don't care to try. If we let a woman sit at this table, there won't be a place left in River Bluff where an old fart will be able to cut loose."

Cole laughed out loud as Knut's statement was met with tacit agreement from the rest of the guys. Jake opened the box, nodded toward his kitchen, where an old refrigerator rattled threateningly but kept cans as cold as mountain snow. "Drinks are in there. Help yourself. But now it's time to pony up, boys. Fifty bucks each for the first tournament."

Each man slid their bills across the table. Jake folded the pile and stuck it in the silver case. "With nine guys, winner gets top prize of two hundred fifty. Second place is one hundred fifty. Third just gets his bankroll back. Same as always." Jake put the dealer's button in front of him. "Host deals first."

"And orders the pizza," Brady added.

"No pizza tonight," Ed said. He pointed to an insulated bag on an end table next to Jake's sofa. "Brought burgers and fries from the café."

Marshall smiled. "I knew there was a reason I liked you, Ed. Now I remember what it was."

Jake finished shuffling and dealt two cards to each

player. Dobbs slid a five-dollar chip to the center of the table, the amount needed to get the betting started. Marshall anted with two-and-a-half dollars, the other forced bet required. Jake nodded at Brady, the first player to decide if he would bet, check or fold.

Brady tossed in a five-dollar chip to equal Dobbs's big blind bet. "I'm in."

Two players dropped out. The rest stayed to see the three-card flop. Jake rolled up a pair of eights and a six for everyone to see. Brady kept his face expressionless. With an eight as one of his hole cards, he was in great shape with three of a kind. When the betting came around to him again, he raised.

Luke studied his face, then mucked his cards. "Brady's got something. He never takes a chance this early in the tournament unless he believes he's got a winner."

Harold Knutson held up a finger. "No table talk about player strategy, Chisum. You know that."

Every private game Brady had ever played in had a rules fanatic. "Lay off, Knut," he said. "You know Luke's never right about anything."

Harold's thick eyebrows came together. "Rules are rules. Either we enforce them or we don't have them. Can't have it both ways."

Luke held up his hands. "Fine. I stand corrected."

Only three players stayed in for the fourth and fifth cards. Brady's threesome held up and he raked in a modest pot.

"You're the luckiest damn player I've ever known," Ed said.

Brady smiled. Luck was relative. "It's early," he said. "You might want to reserve judgment till the end of the night."

Brady misread Cole's play on the next hand. He could have sworn his buddy was bluffing. Cole liked to do that. But he had the nuts flush from the fourth card and slow-played the excellent hand. Four guys stayed in and Cole's winning pot made Brady's look like pocket change.

After forty-five minutes, five guys were left battling for top spots in the first tournament. Marshall had gone all-in, risking what was left of his bankroll with an ace and a king. He'd been beaten by a pair of sixes. Now, with no chips left, out of the tournament, he wandered around the room waiting for the remaining guys to finish. "I'm hungry," he said. "When are we going to eat?"

"Help yourself," Ed said, scratching his head as he contemplated Brady's raise on the table. "In fact, pass those burgers around. Even in that warming bag, they won't stay hot forever."

"And we're not going to live forever, either," Harold said, scowling. "Make up your mind, Ed. Bet or get off the pot."

Marshall set foil-wrapped packages in front of the four players at the table.

"What's with you tonight, Knut?" Luke said. "You've been harping on everybody."

"We ought to have clear rules, that's all I'm saying. In the pro tournaments, they clock every play so no one takes too long. I could have a nap in the time it takes Ed to decide what to do."

"Then do that," Ed snapped. "We'd all rather you were sleeping than complaining. We'll wake you up when it's your turn to bet."

That response brought a few chuckles and made Knut's face redden.

"Besides," Luke said, "if you were paying attention instead of griping, you'd know that every time Ed takes this long he's got shit for cards."

The room hushed. "Damn it, Luke," Knut hollered. "I told you once tonight." He stood up and grabbed his hamburger. "Why don't you stuff your face with this and shut up." He threw the sandwich across the table. It struck Luke in his chest. The wrapping fell off and ketchup splattered on Luke's white denim shirt. The rest of the burger fell in his lap.

Brady stared in shock. This was bad. Most guys could take some ribbing, and Luke could most of the time, but Brady held his breath. His friend looked pissed. Luke started to rise, but was stopped by Dobbs's hands on his shoulders. "Settle down, son," Dobbs said.

"What the hell's the matter with you?" Luke said to Knut. "You crazy or something?"

Knut leaned back in his seat. "Sorry. I had a fight with Sally before I left home. It was a bad one."

"That's no excuse—"

"I know." Knut looked at Ed. "I don't suppose you've got an extra burger in there. Luke's wearing mine."

Luke strained against Dobbs's hold. The room remained hushed. Everyone knew that if Luke wanted to take this to the next level, Dobbs couldn't hold him. No one person in the room could if Luke was determined to settle the score. And then a sputter of suppressed laughter broke the tense silence. Ed looked over at Marshall. "Hap's burger is still in the bag," he said, struggling to contain his laughter. "I don't suppose he'd mind if our buddy Knut here ate it…seeing as how Knut's flew out of his hand like that."

Brady reached over and pulled a pickle off Luke's chest. He glanced down at the burger still covering Luke's crotch. "We could have him come over here and eat this one. Luke's keeping it nice and warm."

Luke speared him a threatening look. "That's not funny."

"Oh, come on. It is a little," Brady said.

Ed's laughter was contagious and soon all the guys joined in. Dobbs released Luke. Jake brought paper towels from the kitchen and Knut placed a cold beer in front of Luke. "Don't know what got into me," he said.

"I'm chocking it up to that case of mad cow disease we all figured you contracted," Luke said.

Knut took the last burger from the bag. "Still, rules are rules…"

Luke's temples literally throbbed. Brady pointed

a finger at Knut. "I wouldn't go there if you know what's good for you. You're on your own now."

Knut dropped the subject. Play continued amiably for the next hour. Jake won the first tournament with Brady coming in second. With six guys left, Brady was holding his own as the next tournament progressed.

Ed Falconetti, who'd been bested with Dobbs's straight draw, came in from having a cigarette. He stopped behind Brady and looked over his shoulder. "So how is that poker-playing girl working out for you?"

Brady rechecked his hole cards, studied the flop again. He didn't want to make a mistake and the mention of Molly suddenly made that more likely. "Fine."

"I met her at the hoedown. She's cute. I could use her at the café."

Brady slid a few chips into the pot. "Forget it."

"I'm not asking you. I'll ask her."

"She's not available."

"Says who?"

"Says me. She's working for us."

"What? That bet thing you've got going on? That's not gainful employment."

Brady looked at Marshall. "Tell him, Dad. Apparently Falconetti's not content to take my word for it."

Marshall shrugged. "Brady's right. Molly is the new bookkeeper at the ranch. Serafina hired her. She's bugging us all to clean up our accounting."

"That's no fun for a pretty woman," Ed said. "Beth

Ann quit on me yesterday and I need to fill her place. Molly told me she used to be a waitress."

Brady ruffled his chips, an impatient gesture he'd picked up a long time ago. "Used to be. She's not anymore. We just told you."

"I think I'll call her tomorrow, make her an offer."

Brady glared up at Ed. "Are you deaf? She's not for hire."

Ed stepped back. "Whoa! Point taken. You're touchy on the subject. Looks like there might be more than poker coaching going on over at Cross Fox."

Brady would have gone to the mat for any of these guys for almost any reason. But tonight a few of them were bugging the hell out of him. He continued staring at Ed. "Check out that bag you brought, Ed. Maybe there's one more burger in there that'll match that classy outfit you're wearing. Because you keep this up, you and Luke are going to walk out of here as the ketchup twins."

Ed grinned. "Just getting the lay of the land on this wager thing," he said. "I'm satisfied. Now, bet or fold. It's getting late."

BRADY LEFT THE WILD CARD shortly after midnight. He was ahead for the night. Not bad considering his mind hadn't been on the game for much of the three and a half hours they played. His dad and Dobbs had left before him, and with their twenty-minute lead time, they were surely home by now and probably snoring soundly.

He cranked up the radio and thrummed his fingers on the steering wheel in time to Kenny Chesney. His pickup flew over the blacktop, but after having only two beers early in the evening, Brady was in control.

Twin lamps illuminated the iron gate at the entrance to Cross Fox. Brady pressed a button on his remote control, and the gates swung wide. He drove in. The lights were still on in the main house, on both levels. Unusual.

But that wasn't what interested him most. Lights in the apartment above the tack room spilled onto the landing outside the door. Molly was obviously still up. "Don't even think about it, Carrick," Brady said to himself as he drove around the circular drive. "It's twelve-thirty, for Pete's sake." As he headed toward the garage, he saw his father storm out of the house toward the stables. Brady cut the engine and jumped out of the truck. "Where are you headed at this hour?"

"Up to the apartment."

"You're going to see Molly?"

"I expect I will. Assuming she's there."

Brady grabbed his arm. "What for?"

Marshall scrubbed his hand down his face. "Because your mother's up there, probably pie-eyed."

"What makes you think that?"

"One of the grooms saw your mother go up to the apartment about three hours ago." He cleared his throat. "Said she had something in her hand."

"A bottle?"

"What else?"

"Has she been drinking today?"

Marshall looked at him as if he was dense. "Actually, I never saw her. She was still in bed when I left the house at noon to run errands. And when I checked on her before leaving for the poker game, Serafina said she was out."

"She was driving?"

"Her car was gone. And I couldn't reach her on her cell phone." He patted his shirt pocket over the outline of his own phone. "I've been half expecting the state police to call me all night."

"Don't jump to conclusions." It was great advice, except Brady wasn't buying it himself. They headed together at a brisk pace toward the stables. "Molly doesn't drink much," Brady said.

"That makes one of them." Marshall's gaze remained fixed on the stairs. "I just hope that poor girl isn't having to put up with..." He stopped, as if the admission was too difficult to utter. "I kept her under control when we had the party, but I haven't been around much the past couple of days."

Marshall took the stairs ahead of Brady. "Have you told Molly about your mother?" he asked. "Warned her?"

"I didn't think I needed to. Mom's...problem...was pretty evident the day Molly arrived." He stepped around his father and rapped on the door. "Molly?"

"Angela?" Marshall hollered. "I know you're in there. Open up."

Brady saw movement in the living room. Molly

walked toward the door, clutching a soft robe close around her. She put a finger to her lips and pointed to the bedroom. "Sam's asleep," she mouthed, and Brady sensed she wanted to tag on *you idiot.*

She opened the door and let them in. "I guess the poker game's over."

"Where's my wife?" Marshall said. He spotted her the same time Brady did—at the game table. She was wearing jeans and a sweatshirt advertising a San Antonio festival from a few years ago. Brady didn't remember ever seeing it before. Her hair was tied back with a simple ribbon. She looked almost like a teenager.

Angela stared up at her husband. "Marshall, what are you doing here?"

He fumbled for words and finally said, "Do you know what time it is?"

"No. What time is it?"

He looked at his bare arm. "Left my damn watch in the bathroom." He spun around to Brady. "Son?"

"It's past twelve-thirty, Dad."

"Twelve-thirty, Angela," Marshall repeated in a gruff voice. "Twelve-thirty."

She smiled benignly up at him. "Am I past curfew?"

"Why did you come up here?"

She glanced down at the table. For the first time Brady noticed cards spread out, two at each chair, three in the middle. "Isn't it obvious?" Angela said.

Brady stepped closer. "You two are playing poker?"

"Yes. Molly's winning. What do I owe you so far, dear?"

Molly consulted a tablet on the table. "Four brownies, two bags of chips, a carton of Mountain Dew and a haircut with Sally Knutson, whoever she is."

Angela frowned up at her husband. "I hope you did better tonight than I'm doing. I'm afraid I'll bankrupt us at this rate."

Brady burst out laughing, only gaining control when Molly shushed him again.

Marshall stared down. He picked up a mug on the table, sniffed the contents. "Have you been...?"

"Drinking?" Angela filled in for him. "What does it smell like?"

He looked puzzled, inhaled again. "Tea."

"Then, yes, you caught me. I've been drinking." She stood up, retrieved her jacket from the back of the chair, her movements sure and precise. "It is late," she said to Molly. "I didn't realize. I've enjoyed myself."

"Me, too," Molly said. "Come back anytime. And it would be okay if you brought another pie."

Marshall followed Angela to the door. "Pie?"

"Banana cream," she said. "I made it this afternoon and brought it over here thinking Molly and Sam might like it. We got to talking and, well, I lost a fortune." She smiled at Marshall. "There's a slice for you in the refrigerator at home if you want it."

He narrowed his eyes. "You made a pie?"

She laughed softly. "Don't sound so surprised, Marsh. I used to bake lots of pies."

"Well, sure, but—"

"Do you want a slice or not?"

He grinned. "Oh, angel, I want it."

After they left, Brady stared at Molly. "Poker?"

She nodded.

"Somehow I don't believe that's the whole story."

She walked to the sofa. "It isn't, exactly." Reaching under a couch cushion she brought out an unopened bottle of wine. "Your mother brought this along with the pie. It's like she told you. One thing led to another. We got to talking, gorged ourselves on pie...." She gave Brady a smart-alecky smile. "I know what you're thinking, but Sam had already gone to bed. He didn't have pie."

"I wasn't thinking that. I'm just amazed the bottle's still corked."

She handed it to him. "Do with it what you please. I served tea and Angela drank it. We had a great time. But neither one of us is any good at poker—yet."

"I don't know about that. You're getting a Sally Knutson haircut."

Molly started to sweep the cards into a stack.

"Wait a minute. Is there any pie left?"

"A slice or two."

He took off his jacket and sat at the table. "Then deal me in. One hand. All or nothing."

Ten minutes later, Brady licked the rest of the creamy banana filling from his fork and laid the utensil in the empty pie plate. "I'd forgotten how good my mother's pie was. It's been a long time since she made one."

"Maybe she just needed an incentive," Molly said.

"I think Angela wants to be appreciated for her talents, even pie-making. She really is a charming woman."

"When she's…" Brady stopped. He should be celebrating this moment, not dredging up a reason to ruin it. He sat back in his chair and smiled. "Thanks."

"Don't mention it. We had fun."

Brady eyed his jacket on the sofa but was reluctant to get up and put it on. He watched Molly across the table as she gathered up the cards and chips and put things in order—a sign that he should leave. He didn't want to. Her skin glowed in the low light. Her hair curled delicately over her shoulders. And she'd relaxed her death grip on the robe so the lapels parted, revealing a hint of something lacy underneath. He fisted his hand to keep from reaching out a finger and tracing a line above the fabric.

She broke the spell by clasping the robe again. "What are you looking at?"

"You," he said truthfully. "I'm thinking…about kissing you."

He waited. No reaction, so he said, "And suddenly I feel like a jackass."

He thought she almost smiled. "Thinking about kissing me makes you a jackass?"

"No. Not going through with it does." He crossed his arms. "Hell, let's just do it and get it over with."

Her eyebrows arched. "I don't think so."

"It'll make us both feel better."

She placed her palms flat on the table, revealing a sliver of lace. "I don't need that to make me feel good."

She was lying. Her breasts rose and fell sharply with each intake of breath; her skin flushed. He felt an immediate reaction in the tightness of his jeans.

Get up, Brady, he said to himself. *Go around the table, lift her to her feet and kiss her.* All at once, he resented the hell out of that stupid bet.

"It's late," she said. "You'd better go. I'll see you tomorrow."

"I won't be here tomorrow. I've got to pick up a three-year-old at the Lone Star Park racetrack outside Dallas."

Did he imagine a flicker of disappointment in her eyes?

"Oh. Then I'll see you Friday."

He rose, put on his jacket. "Right."

A few seconds later, when Brady ran his tongue over his lips as he went down the stairs, he still tasted his mother's pie. But now it didn't nearly satisfy him. He could think of something that would have been a whole lot better.

From a crack in the door, Molly watched him cross the yard in the glow of the security lights. She unfastened the tie at her waist, let the robe part. A cool breath of air fanned her chest. She reminded herself why she was here, what Brady had done to her and Sam. And it occurred to her that by staying at Cross Fox, she ran the risk of losing some of the pleasure in revenge. She couldn't let that happen. Still, Thursday, with Brady in Dallas, seemed like it would be a long day.

CHAPTER TEN

AT ONE-THIRTY on Friday afternoon Molly closed the ledger and returned it to the kitchen pantry. She had an hour until Sam got out of school and there was something she wanted to do before she left the ranch.

She found Serafina in the sunroom. "I'm through for today," Molly said. "I'm going back to the apartment."

"Before you go, you need to write yourself a paycheck."

"It can wait. I've only worked five days. Twenty-five hours, actually."

"Nonsense. Everyone here gets paid on Fridays. Follow me."

Serafina went down the hallway and entered a small, dark-paneled, masculine office. Opening a desk drawer, she pulled out a checkbook. "Mr. Carrick always leaves a few signed checks on Friday if he's not going to be here. He also left a new-employee form for you to fill out.

Remembering that Serafina had suggested a rate of eight dollars an hour, Molly said, "I've earned two hundred dollars this week. I'll have to calculate the payroll taxes, medicare payment and social security." Molly sat at Marshall's desk and applied her deductions to her gross pay. "Looks like I'll net $172.16."

Serafina flipped open the check record. "Fine. Write that amount and take it."

Molly thanked Serafina and headed out, the check tucked securely in the pocket of her jeans. It wasn't a lot of money, but Molly was thankful to get it. So far, in the week she'd lived at Cross Fox, she'd spent nearly fifty dollars. Serafina had told her the day they went shopping that Brady insisted on taking care of her board, and since then, Molly had given the housekeeper a list of the essentials she needed in her kitchen. But she hadn't included luxury food items, snacks or drinks that Sam liked. She paid for those out of her own money. Plus, she'd purchased school supplies on Monday. But she was satisfied that her bookkeeping job would keep her savings intact, at least for a while and, along with learning poker techniques, keep her busy.

She went into her apartment, transferred the check to her wallet and sat on the sofa with the portable phone on her lap. She'd postponed making this call for days and couldn't put it off any longer. She punched in the number to the Good Shepherd Baptist Church office.

"Pastor Whelan," her father said.

"Hi, Dad. It's me."

"Molly Jean," he said simply, his tone expressionless.

"How are you?"

"How do you think I am?" he said, lowering his

voice as if he didn't want anyone to hear him. "Worried sick about what happened to you two. Trying to minister to my parishoners while I keep up the house on my own and explain to everyone why my daughter left and gave me no idea where she is."

"You know where I am, Dad. I told you and Uncle Cliff I was going to San Antonio."

"To be with friends, you said."

"Yes."

"You don't have any friends in San Antonio, Molly."

That may have been true at first, but it wasn't anymore. She almost had friends. There was Becky Howard and Serafina. And maybe even Fran Wardell and Angela. "I do, Dad. I have friends here."

"Then why haven't I heard from you? Don't these friends have telephones?"

"Of course. And I have my cell phone on all the time. You have the number."

"I'm not going to call you. I'm not the one who left."

She sighed. "Okay, but we're talking now. Sam and I have settled in and I wanted to let you know how we're doing."

She thought just maybe he'd express concern about her, but he said, "How is my grandson?"

"He's fine. You don't have to worry about him."

"How can I not worry? You uprooted him from his home."

"He's happy, Dad. He's in school. His teacher is—"

"Do you even have a place to live?"

"Of course. I'm calling from my apartment. Let me give you the phone number here."

"I don't need it. Anything I have to say to you, I can say right now."

She sat straight, steeling herself. "All right."

"I want you to come home before this irrational behavior goes on too long. I know I said I wouldn't take you in again, but I've had time to reconsider. If you return now I'll forgive you this transgression and we'll go back to the way things were. You were safe here. You had a roof over your head—Sam had his routine."

Molly blinked back tears. That's what he thought a man should provide, the necessities of life. That's why her mother had left. Those things only kept the body alive. "I know, Dad, but that's not all I want now. You have to accept it."

After a short silence, he said, "You're just like your mother. Always wanting more. That selfish attitude may satisfy your cravings for a time, but consider what you're doing to the boy."

"I think about Sam all the time. I never make a decision without taking his welfare into consideration."

"You're certainly not doing that now."

His words cut like a knife. He'd never tried to understand her needs and dreams, just like he'd never tried to understand her mother. Even now he only cared about how Sam was.

"You can still make the right decision, Molly Jean," he said. "Come home."

She paused, waiting for him to say something

about how important she was to him beyond her ability to keep his house in order. Would he tell her that he wanted her back as much as he wanted Sam? She knew the answer and he confirmed it when he added, "My heart suffers when I think about my grandchild, and you've only compounded your past sins by keeping him away from his home."

Molly filled her lungs with what she hoped was courage. "We're not returning to Prairie Bend, Dad. I'm sorry if that hurts you. I don't want you out of our lives. I never did. I appreciate everything you've done for me..."

"Is this the way you show appreciation, by embarrassing me in front of my congregation again, just like your—"

His voice hitched, and Molly felt overwhelmingly sad for him. "I never meant to do that, Dad."

"I'm giving you one last opportunity to do the right thing, Molly. I raised you to be a God-fearing woman who respects herself and honors her parent. But time and again you've flaunted me and the values I've tried to instill in you. You took up with that—that *cowboy* when I told you nothing good would come of it. He was gone more than he was home, leaving you and Sam to fend for yourselves."

Molly's chest tightened. Her father would never have approved of any man unless he'd picked him for her. She had to force her next words past the painful constriction in her lungs. "And I've told you, Dad, don't talk about Kevin."

He breathed heavily into the phone. "This is it, Molly. Come home. There won't be any more chances."

Her fingers squeezed the receiver. "I have to go, Dad. I'm sorry. Take care of yourself." She gently placed the phone into its cradle, pressed her hand over her chest and filled her lungs with air. "You have to make this work, Molly." She had to do this for Kevin, for Sam…for herself. Her father was right. There was no going back. Brady Carrick, the man who changed her past would be the one to give her a future. She just had to take it from him.

She stood and went to the door, her gaze automatically drawn to the driveway where she thought she might see the pickup truck and trailer. Brady had a home to come to. Molly didn't. But that would change. She would make a home for herself and her son, and she would do it by becoming the best darn poker player Brady could teach her to be.

Brady arrived home at about six. Molly was putting her supper dishes away when she saw his truck pull around the back of the house. Two hours later the telephone in the apartment rang. "Hey, Molly," Brady said. "You up for poker?"

All about the game, Molly reminded herself to erase the effect of his voice vibrating in the pit of her stomach, the memory of his smile. "Sure, but none of this skirting the real issue anymore," she said. "I know the vocabulary and the cards that have the best chance of taking pots. Tonight let's get down to what'll make me win."

He chuckled. "Serious stuff, eh? What'd you have in mind?"

"Let's talk strategy, statistics, money management. How long until the tournament?"

"Less than four weeks now."

"Good. In four weeks I want to know what you know."

"I'll be there in ten minutes."

Molly brought a soda to the living room and handed it to Sam. "It's Friday night. You don't have to go to bed early."

He sipped his drink. "Can I watch one of my movies?"

"Yep. Pick a long one if you want."

He flipped through a box of DVDs, chose *Cars,* his favorite, and slipped it into the player. He sat on the sofa, his stockinged feet on the coffee table, his cotton pony beside him. Molly put on her oldest, most comfortable sweater and buttoned it to her throat. She popped some corn, set a bowl in front of Sam and put another one in the middle of the game table. Yes, it was all about the game, but it didn't hurt to have the proper distractions to help her remember that. She was only human after all.

MOLLY SLEPT LATE on Sunday morning, not rising until almost nine o'clock. She'd gone into town on Saturday to the local bookstore and purchased a book on Texas Hold 'Em. Using the skills Brady had taught her and the advice of the author, a two-time World Series of Poker finalist, she memorized the statistical odds of various hole card combinations. She'd planned to impress Brady with her new knowledge on Saturday night, but he'd left the ranch about eight o'clock and hadn't returned by the time she went to bed at midnight. As she prepared breakfast for Sam and sipped her coffee, she tried to tell herself she wasn't at all curious about where he'd been.

Sam carried his Pop-Tarts into the living room and looked out the window. "I see Dodger, Mom. Can I go outside?"

Molly joined him at the window. The Jack Russell terrier was bounding after Dobbs in front of the stables. "I guess so," she said. "But remember what I told you. Don't bother the men if they're working and stay away from the horses."

Sam ran into the bedroom and returned with his jacket. "I know what you told me, but I want to see Amber Mac."

"No, Sam. When I told you to avoid horses, I especially meant Amber Mac. He's not used to children."

Sam zipped his jacket. "Right. He has strings on him."

"What?"

"You said he had strings."

She recalled her initial warning to Sam about the new colt. "What I said was he's high-strung. That means he's excitable. I understand most racehorses are. That's why they don't make good pets for children."

He pouted, but said, "Okay. I'll just play with Dodger."

"That's fine. Go ahead and I'll be there in a few minutes."

Molly watched him descend the stairs and call to the dog. Soon Sam was laughing, Dodger was yipping, and they were both running in the grass. Molly went to the kitchen, cleared the dishes and then dressed in a pair of jeans and a light blue jersey knit top. After clasping her necklace, she checked in the mirror to see that the turquoise charm was centered on her chest. The unusual design of a Navajo basket with Sam's birthstone in the middle had been a gift from Kevin when Sam was born, and she'd rarely gone a day without wearing it. She pulled her hair into a ponytail, slipped into a fleece Windbreaker and left the apartment.

She wasn't overly concerned when she didn't see Sam playing by the statue. But when Dodger trotted out of a stall without him she began to feel alarmed. She hollered her son's name while heading to the nearest stall. She checked several, all the while calling for Sam. Finally she heard an answer.

"I'm in here, Mom."

She found him in a large room that opened onto a breezeway, separating the stables down the middle. A dozen buckets sat in front of him and he was pouring pellets into one of them with a large scoop. She stopped in the doorway. "What are you doing?"

"Shh, Mom, you'll make me lose count." He emptied the scoop into the bucket. "That makes two of those." Next he picked up a smaller scoop and filled it with pellets of a different color. Dumping the contents into the same bucket, he said, "And one of those." He reached into the bucket and swirled the nuggets around with his hand.

"Sam, I asked you what you're doing."

"I'm feeding the horses," he said, pointing to a very large tub behind him. "I've got to put two from this one..." he pointed to another large tub "...and one from this one in each bucket and stir everything up. That's what the horses eat."

"Who told you to?"

"Mr. Carrick...Brady. He said my weight wasn't good so I had to do this."

"He said that?"

Sam went to the first tub, dipped the scoop inside and returned to the feed bucket.

"Put that scoop down," Molly said.

"No, Mom. Brady said—"

"I don't care what he said. Stop doing that and tell me where Brady is."

"He's right here."

Molly gasped at the sound of the deep baritone voice coming from directly behind her. Her shoulder collided with Brady's chest when she spun around. Instead of stepping back, he smiled. "You looking for me?"

She took a breath, calming her escalating anger and another equally strong emotion she shouldn't be feeling. "I certainly am." She pushed him back into the breezeway and lowered her voice to a growl. "How dare you comment on my son's weight? I told you that topic was out of bounds."

He barked his disbelief. "What? I never said anything of the sort."

Molly stared through the doorway at Sam. "What did you tell me, honey? Why did Mr. Carrick say you had to work?"

Sam wrinkled his nose and looked at Brady. "I kinda forget. What *did* you tell me?"

Brady thought a moment before a grin spread across his face. "I said that here on a ranch everyone has to pull his weight. Do you know what that means?"

Sam shook his head.

"It means what you're doing now. It takes a lot of manpower to keep up with the work on a place like this. Every last guy has to do what he can."

At that moment Dobbs walked in, said good morning and went into another room.

Brady nodded at his retreating figure. "From the oldest cuss on Cross Fox to the youngest." He pointed at Sam. "That's you."

Sam emptied feed into a bucket and returned for more. "Oh, that's right. I remember now."

"So how are you doing?" Brady asked him.

"I'm doing good. Two scoops, then one scoop. Just like you told me."

Brady looked into the bucket. "Yep. That seems about right to me. When you finish that, I've got a horse I'd like you to brush down. Think you can handle that?"

Sam beamed. "A real horse?"

"That's all we've got here," Brady said. He took Molly by the arm and steered her away from the feed room. "A man's working here, Molly. You and I should leave him alone."

Molly's initial inclination to apologize vanished. As soon as they were out of hearing, she turned on Brady. "What do you think you're doing?"

He pushed his hat back and scratched his head. "I just told you. Explained everything."

"And I told you. Sam is not part of this arrangement we have."

His eyes narrowed. "I'm not trying to cut in on your parenting, Molly. I just figured—"

"The heck you're not. You've got him working, tending live animals—"

"*Chores,* Molly. They're called chores, and I did them when I was younger than Sam is now."

"Sam isn't you, Brady. He's never been around horses. You think just because he carries around that stuffed animal he knows enough to get close to a real horse?"

"No. I think that throwing a stick for that silly dog isn't enough for any boy. He needs to feel useful, to have a purpose."

Molly fisted her hands at her sides. "He's a child, Brady. You make him sound like a senior citizen on the verge of retirement! Besides, how would you know what my son needs? You don't know him beyond a quick trip to the medical center and few critical remarks about his weight."

"And speaking of that, I thought that working a few pounds off around the stables couldn't hurt him…."

Molly sucked in a breath and opened her mouth. Brady wisely switched topics. "Look," he said, "I saw the kid out here a few minutes ago and I figured I'd give him something to do. If I stepped on your mommy toes, I'm sorry." He rubbed his neck, gave her a contrite grin. "I seem to be saying that a lot these days. I'll lay off. No interference from this point on."

Suddenly she felt foolish. There was nothing wrong with Brady's attempts to include Sam in ranch activities—in theory and under strict supervision. But he had to know that he couldn't make decisions involving her son without talking to her first. Sam was all she had. She'd lost everything else. If anything happened to Sam…Molly squeezed her eyes shut, getting control of emotions that were dangerously close to revealing more of herself than she wanted to.

Brady touched her elbow. "What's wrong now? I said I was sorry."

She slowly opened her eyes. "I just want you to understand…."

"I do. If I come up with any more bright ideas concerning your kid, I'll check with you first."

She tried to smile. "That's all I'm asking."

Dobbs came around a corner. He led an animal on a rope, a creature that looked like a horse, only it was about the size of a large dog. Dobbs handed the animal over to Brady, nodded to Molly and walked away. Molly blinked. "What is that?"

"One of our minis," he said. "We have four miniature horses at Cross Fox. Mom loves them. They're like pets."

The horse, brown with a white blaze on its nose to match its long tail, stood no higher than Molly's waist. "I've heard of miniatures, but I've never seen one. Is it a baby?"

Brady chuckled. "No. In fact, this is the oldest mini on the ranch. Ebeneezer is twelve. He's great company for the thoroughbreds. And…" he patted the animal's rump "…he's the horse I was going to have Sam groom this morning."

Now she really did feel like a fool. "Sam would like that," she said. "I had no idea you meant a horse this size."

Brady frowned. "You thought I was going to turn the care of a seventeen-hand thoroughbred over to an inexperienced child?"

"I might have jumped to the wrong conclusion, but I'm the only one Sam has watching out for him. I have to keep him safe."

"Well, sure. But there's such a thing as being too protective."

She bristled again. "A parent can't be too protective. Especially when her son is hanging around someone who's never had children."

She was sorry she'd said that. She only assumed

Brady hadn't had a child. She didn't know for sure. And anyway, it was an overly critical comment.

Brady stroked Ebeneezer's nose. "If there's one thing I've learned Molly, it's that nobody should tackle a task he's not prepared for, whether it's brushing down a horse or making a bet that's too big for his bankroll. I wouldn't let Sam bite off more than he can chew."

Right. Molly knew that Brady had allowed—no *encouraged*—a starstruck cowboy to play well beyond his means in a poker game in Vegas. Where had Brady's noble sentiments been that night?

Sam ran into the breezeway. "I've got all those buckets filled," he hollered. Then, catching sight of Ebeneezer, he skidded to a stop. "What the heck is that?"

"What's it look like?" Brady said.

"Like a horse, only…"

"Smaller?"

"Way smaller. Can I touch it?"

Brady looked at Molly. She nodded.

Sam put his hand on Ebeneezer's back. "Look at me, Mom," he said. "I'm not a bit afraid of this horse." He looked up at Brady. "Can I ride him?"

"First things first, cowboy," Brady said. "You've got to get to know him before you mount up." He turned to Molly. "What do you say? Can I introduce these two fellas?"

"Sure."

Brady led the horse to the stable with Sam jogging

along beside him. Molly followed at a distance. "The way you get to know a horse is with a bucket of feed and a curry brush," Brady said. "You think you can handle that?"

"Yep."

"Here at Cross Fox we work our way up with horses and eventually get to the saddle part."

Molly stood outside as Brady attached two ropes to Ebeneezer's halter and fixed them to chains on each side of the wide opening. The horse, now unable to walk away, stood patiently as Brady handed Sam a brush and demonstrated how to smooth it over the animal's coat. Sam soon had the rhythm of the job.

Two emotions warred within her. She was grateful to see Sam so enthusiastic about something, but she couldn't shake the feeling that Brady had once again managed to demonstrate her ineptitude as a parent. She was here to learn poker from him, not how to be a better mother to Sam. She already believed she was darned near perfect at that job. It was the one she'd committed her life to. How the heck could she not resent Brady for acting like it was so easy?

CHAPTER ELEVEN

MOLLY PICKED Sam up at school on Friday and bought a pizza they could warm up later for dinner. On the way home he chattered nonstop about the upcoming weekend and how he could brush down Ebeneezer again. That was his reward for filling the feed buckets every afternoon this week.

The chore Brady had assigned him was becoming automatic now. Sam fetched the buckets himself, took them to the outdoor spigot where he rinsed each one clean of the residue left from the morning feed. Then he dried them and filled them with grain. He still wasn't allowed to hang the buckets inside the stalls—one of the stable hands did that—but Sam, struggling valiantly with the weight of each bucket, left one in front of each door.

"I've got to bunk down early tonight," Sam said as Molly drove through the iron gates to Cross Fox property.

She smiled at the lingo Sam had picked up from the stable hands. "Why's that?"

"Brady's always up before me. I don't want him to give my job to someone else."

"Okay, then. Nine o'clock should be a good bedtime for you. Just remember to have your bath earlier than usual."

Molly wasn't worried anymore about being alone with Brady in the living room after Sam went to bed. They'd kept an appropriate distance from each other every time they'd met this week. The poker lessons had become intense and Molly had to focus all her attention on learning the intricacies of the game. Between what Brady was telling her and what she'd learned from the book, her head was spinning and she didn't have time to think about Brady—too much. Tournament-play poker wasn't a game for the faint of heart, especially now that she was learning about finesse and game psychology.

The seriousness of her task became even more significant when Brady told her he'd sent in her entry fee for the quarter finals in Vegas. In addition to her board at Cross Fox, he'd invested one thousand in fees and a couple hundred in hotel reservations, making their bet more real. And the possibility of the negotiated fifty-fifty split of that several thousand dollar payoff was another darned good incentive.

Molly kept telling herself she should be happy with their new, more serious mentor/protégée relationship, and she was. But deep down there was a part of her, that part her father always criticized as being outrageous and unbridled, that missed Brady's flirting. *You can't have it both ways, Molly Jean. Brady is still the same man who was in that Vegas bar.*

She pulled up in front of the apartment and rubbed her arms as she got out of the car. The wind was biting. "We'll have to turn the heat up tonight," she said to Sam. And after Sam had gone to sleep, well, there were other, more interesting ways to keep warm. But she'd just have to stop thinking about those.

BRADY ARRIVED at 8:30 p.m., too late for pizza, but not for the apple pie he brought with him. Melted butter glistened on the ruffled crust. Molly inhaled cinnamon, spicy and warm. She took the plate from his hands. "Angela again?"

"Who else? My mother has become Betty Crocker lately. Not that I'm complaining." He smiled. "And neither is my dad. I never knew pie could have such a positive effect on his mood."

"I can believe it of this pie. But are you sure his good mood is all about baking?" she asked.

"No. But I'm not going to overanalyze a good thing."

She sent a playful look at his midsection. "If your mother keeps this up, there will be two cowboys around here who'll need to slim down to get into their britches."

He grinned. "Where's my partner in calorie abuse?"

She pointed to the bedroom. "Reading, would you believe. He checked out a couple of books from the school library today. You can probably guess the subject."

"I'm thinking it's four-legged."

Molly set the warm pie on the game table and

went into the kitchen for plates, forks and a serving knife. She'd seen Angela twice this week. They'd gone to the supermarket together, a chore Angela said she'd left up to Ruby for too long. And Angela had taken her into River Bluff to meet a few of the merchants who hadn't attended the hoedown. Molly was introduced to several of the waitresses at The Longhorn and Sally Knutson at the beauty shop. Sally gave her an expert's opinion on the haircut she would advise when Molly was ready to collect on her bet with Angela.

"So how is your mother today?" Molly asked when she came back to the living room.

"She's better than she has been for quite a while. I might have you to thank for that. You and Sam have been a positive influence on her. She enjoys cooking again and loved taking you into town. I can't say she's given up her bad habit entirely, but she's trying."

"And is your father helping?"

Brady cut a wedge of pie and slid it onto a plate. "As much as he's capable. He doesn't see my mother's problem as any reflection on him."

"But you do?"

"Yeah. Except maybe I'm not the right person to judge. My father has certain standards that can be hard to meet. You must have noticed that Marshall Carrick is slightly larger-than-life."

She thought about her own father and couldn't help comparing the two men. Marshall was willing to let his son follow his ambitions, strive for his goals. He'd forgiven Brady for past mistakes and he seemed on the verge of forgiving Angela hers. Luther always judged, never allowing Molly to move on. "I suppose he is larger-than-life," she said. "But he seems like a good man."

"He is. But he believes there's no avoiding the consequences of the choices a man makes. Once you settle on a decision, it's yours, good or bad, and a real man lives with it and doesn't run away. Dad accepts responsibility for his problems even if he doesn't accept his role in the problems of others."

Molly took the plate Brady offered. "Accepting responsibility is a good thing, isn't it?"

"In theory it is. But along with accepting those bad decisions, I believe a man should recognize the causes. Dad never did that."

Neither did her dad, Molly thought.

"If a horse went lame," Brady continued, "Dad wouldn't consider that it happened because he'd failed to examine the animal closely enough. He just accepted the horse as a burden he had to bear. In the same way, if his wife started drinking too much, he wouldn't think that it was in any way his fault. He would just shoulder the responsibility for her care without wondering if he might be able to do something about it."

For Molly, love and forgiveness went hand in hand. If you loved someone, you forgave them. She sensed that Marshall's capacity to forgive was greater than Luther's. Her father seemed to have forgotten how to forgive when his wife left him. He'd certainly never forgiven his daughter.

"So you think your father is the reason your mother started drinking?" Molly asked.

Brady shrugged. "She told me once in confidence that she no longer felt she was a part of his life, that he didn't see her as an equal. She was merely a decoration on his arm at parties or in the winner's circle at the track." He smiled sadly. "Until he no longer needed her for that."

Molly sighed. "That's a shame. It sounds as if your father was so busy feeling responsible for Angela that he forgot why he married her in the first place."

Brady cut himself a slice of pie and set it on the table. "You're an amazing woman, Molly. I think you've just described what happens to a lot of marriages." He dug his fork into the pie. "And often the mistakes two people make can't be mended."

She and Brady had never talked about his marriage, but Molly knew he'd had a wife. Everyone who owned a TV in the Dallas area knew something of Brady Carrick's private life. At one time the handsome wide receiver for the Cowboys and the stunning woman on his arm had achieved celebrity status, appearing on magazine covers and local talk shows. She wondered now if he and his wife forgot why they married. Or worse, married for the wrong reasons.

"Hey, Mom, can I have some pie?" said Sam, coming out of the bedroom.

She scooped a slice on a plate and handed it to

him. She smiled to herself when she realized that the helping was rather small, and she wondered at that subconscious decision on her part. "Be sure to thank Mrs. Carrick tomorrow."

Sam sat on the sofa. "I will."

Brady pulled his chair close to the table and dealt two sets of hole cards, one for her and one for him. He turned up three cards in the center for the flop. "You ready?"

"Sure."

"Let's see what we have here. Turn your cards over." She did. Brady kept his hidden. Molly had a pair of nines. The flop was a king, four, eight.

"What would you do, Molly?" he asked.

"With a pair of nines? I'd bet."

"Good decision, but what should you notice immediately about the flop?"

"That the king can be dangerous."

"Exactly. You have the highest pair showing, but with ten players in a game, there's a pretty good chance of somebody having a king in the hole and beating you. Still, it's worth a moderate bet to see what's going on."

He turned the fourth and fifth cards. Molly didn't improve her hand, but another king came up, giving her two pair, nines and kings. Molly admitted she would probably fold. The possibility of that third king showing up in an opponent's hole cards was too great.

"Good choice. But in this case, if it were just between you and me…" he flipped his hole cards over.

He had a Jack and a seven, cards he would surely have mucked if this had been a real game "…you would have won."

She frowned. "I had a feeling I would have. I almost bet my two pairs."

He smiled. "You know what I've told you…."

"You don't need to say it again. Never bet a feeling."

"Right. Instincts can be good. But feelings will kill you."

He didn't have to tell her that. She knew about the devastating consequences of feelings. She learned that lesson a long time ago.

"I'm going to bed, Mom." Sam set his plate on the coffee table.

"Okay, sweetie. Brush your teeth. Your pj's are on your cot. Do you need any help?"

He gave her an obstinate look she rarely saw. "I'm seven, Mom. I don't need help going to bed."

"Of course you don't. I'll see you when you wake up then."

He waved to Brady. "I suppose you'll need me in the morning. We've gotta feed."

Brady smiled. "Absolutely. Bright and early."

Sam went into the bedroom. Molly stared at the closed door and then the pie plate on the table. "I can't get him to take his dirty dishes into the kitchen, and you've got him carting heavy buckets around the stables."

"Bet you could."

"What?"

"Get him to take his dishes into the kitchen." He leaned back. "Try it on me."

She placed a finger on the side of his empty plate, slid it toward him and said without cracking a smile, "You're not leaving this here, are you?"

Brady stood up, grabbed the plate. "No, ma'am. Not when you put it like that." He picked up her plate and Sam's, as well, and took the whole stack into the kitchen. When he came back he said, "See? It's usually only a matter of asking."

She'd never have thought to ask her father to take his dishes to the sink. For that matter, she'd never asked Kevin to. Now that she thought about it, she'd been carrying other people's dirty dinnerware for years. No wonder she rather enjoyed watching Brady take over the chore, even if he was only teasing her. "Point taken."

"You're the boss of the kid, Molly. You're the adult."

Right. Again Brady makes parenting sound so easy.

"Speaking of Sam," she said. "Are you going to let him ride Ebeneezer?"

"That's a tough one. I might let him sit on him, but Ebeneezer's not cut out for carrying passengers."

"He's too small?"

"Yeah, and too old. I'd maybe let him carry forty pounds or so, but Sam's too heavy." He stopped, obviously aware that he was broaching a taboo subject. "I didn't mean anything by that."

"It's all right. He'll be disappointed, that's all."

"We use boys for training here, though. We like to

introduce the thoroughbreds to weight on their backs early on, before they take a saddle. I've been hiring Becky Howard's son, Shane, to sit on the horses. That's all he does for now, just sits on them. It's safe, because Dobbs and I hold the animals the whole time but you never know when a horse might act up."

"Sam's not old enough for that job."

"No, I don't think he is, and since I'm responsible for you two, I wouldn't want anything to happen."

His statement startled her in light of what he'd just said about his father's strong sense of responsibility. "You're not responsible for my son," she said. "I am. Only me."

"Well, sure, but I'm the reason he's here. I offered you that bet."

"You're not your father, Brady. The decision to go ahead with this bet was mine at least as much as yours. And once the decision was made, it didn't mean you had to shoulder the burden of this choice forever or make decisions about the welfare of me or my son. When this is over, we'll be fine." *It's not like what happened in Las Vegas. You didn't talk me into doing something I didn't want to do or shouldn't have done. It's not as if I'm going to kill myself when this ends—or even be sad.*

A frown pulled at his lips as he stared at her for a long moment.

"Do you want to say something?" she asked.

"Maybe now's not the time."

She wondered if what she'd said had somehow

insulted him. She couldn't imagine why. He'd made it clear from the day they met that he wanted her gone when the bet was over. She pushed the cards toward him. "A few more hands? Test my decision-making?"

He shuffled. "Okay."

When he dealt her two hole cards, he said, "I believe you, you know that?"

"You do? About what?"

"I don't doubt that you and Sam will be fine no matter what you decide to do after this."

If everything turns out the way it's supposed to. She peeked at her cards. "You want to see them?"

"No. Bet or fold on your own this time. And prepare yourself. In a little while I'm going to teach you something that has absolutely nothing to do with poker."

Intrigued, she looked up at him. "Or horses?"

"Or horses." He tapped the side of his head. "I do have a vast storehouse of fairly worthless junk up here that isn't related to racing or gambling."

She nodded toward his coat draped over the arm of the sofa. "Does it have anything to do with whatever you hid under your jacket when you came in?"

He grinned. "You don't miss anything, do you?"

"Try not to."

"Amazing."

AN HOUR LATER, Brady stood up from the table, stretched, and suggested Molly do the same. "You might want to limber up," he said. "We've been sitting a long time."

She shot him a look that said don't-mess-with-me. "I need to be limber for what we're going to do?"

"Uh-huh." He went to the bedroom, leaned against the door and listened. "He's sleeping. Wouldn't want the cowpoke to hear all the shenanigans going on out here."

She drummed her fingers on the tabletop. "Brady, I'm probably not going to agree to do anything I don't want my son to hear."

"Oh, you'll want to do this."

She glanced furtively at the jacket. He anticipated her next move just before she lunged. Beating her to the sofa, he scooped the jacket and a videotape he'd hidden underneath to his chest. "Cheater," he said. "Although I must admit, you do seem limber enough."

She poked the jacket. "What's under there?"

"I'll give you a clue. What did we talk about around the time of my dad's party?"

She thought a moment. "I remember telling you to go away."

He recalled their conversation in the kitchen when she was working on the ranch books. "Okay, you did say that, but I'm thinking of something you said the day of the hoedown."

She crossed her arms. "I don't know, Brady. I said a lot of things that day."

He was loving this. He pulled the tape out and threw the jacket on the sofa. "You said you couldn't do the Texas two-step."

She raised her eyebrows. "No, I didn't. I think I said I wasn't in the mood to dance."

"Oh, right, but I accused you of using that as an excuse for not knowing how."

"So you did." She frowned. "Then you'd better tell me that's a movie and not an instructional video."

"Sorry." He turned on the television, slid the tape out of its case and popped it into the cassette player. "It's so easy, Molly, you'll catch on right away. And if you know the two-step you can dance anywhere in Texas. Between this video and what I already know, I'll have you two-stepping all over the dance floor at the Eagle's Nest Casino in Grand Pass."

She coughed. "The what in where?"

He paused the video after the credits. "I forgot to tell you. We're going to the casino about a hundred miles from here at the Mexican border next Saturday. You're going to play poker for real."

"I can't go out of town. What about...?"

Anticipating her reaction, he was ready. "I talked to Serafina today. She can't wait to have Sam stay with her and Dobbs on Saturday. They're planning on taking him into San Antonio to a movie." He grinned. "You wouldn't want to deprive the cowpoke of a night on the town, would you?"

Even mother-of-the-year Molly couldn't find anything objectionable with such well thought out arrangements, so she kept quiet.

"Ready to dance?"

She sighed. "I guess I can try."

He started the tape. A cute blonde in a white halter top and a red skirt with ruffles at the bottom stood next to a guy in a blue Western shirt, jeans and boots. When a guitar and fiddle struck up a slow ballad, the two gently swayed their hips. A narrator with a strong Texas drawl urged everyone to begin with the basic dance position.

Brady placed his right hand on Molly's waist and instructed her to put her left one on his shoulder. They clasped their free hands at the side in classic dance posture. The instructor explained the fundamental move. Molly moved her right foot back and followed it with her left. It was an uncomplicated step-together, step-together. Unfortunately, Molly had a hard time grasping the six-count beat.

Brady shifted his hand to just below her waist. "You gotta sway your hips, Molly." She did, but the action was forced. She reminded Brady of a hula dancer on a car dashboard. "Now move forward," he said. He held her tightly, guiding her through the steps. "Now we're going to turn in a circle."

She stumbled, but he caught her. "I don't know about this," she said. "The guy on the video didn't say we should turn."

"Don't pay any attention to him. He sounds corny. Just listen to the music. Try to feel it."

"All I can feel are my two left feet."

He stepped away from her, turned her around so her back was to his chest and held her hand over her shoulder. "This is called the sweetheart position. It's pretty easy." She felt more like a wooden doll in his arms than a flesh-and-blood woman. He tried to make her more comfortable by leaning close and repeating in a low, calm voice, "Step-together, step-together. Quick, quick. Slow, slow. Relax, Molly. And don't look at your feet. Let your hips follow the beat of the music." He twined her around to face him. "You think you've got it?" He knew she didn't.

"That's all there is?"

"For the most part. The two-step is just a combination of fox-trot and swing. Sort of a Texas-style waltz with an extra kick to it. If I can do it with a bum knee, you shouldn't have any problem."

"Well, heck, anybody can do this," she said.

He didn't share her confidence. He was beginning to wonder if the dance lesson was a good idea. Some people had natural rhythm and some didn't. Molly fell into that latter category. She seemed to be moving to a beat in her own head. So Molly wasn't a dancer. Big deal. Her lack of grace didn't make her feel any less good in his arms. And there was a lot to be said for practice.

But he couldn't believe her boldness when she suddenly looked into his eyes and said, "I think I've got it. I'm ready for that casino dance floor."

You may be ready for one part of the casino, he thought, but the dance floor isn't it. He cleared his throat, figured he'd better not encourage her too much. "Actually there's a lot more to the two-step. There's the crossover, the under-arm twirl and a fairly complicated maneuver where you have to step behind me, kind of waltz under my arm and come around again to the sweetheart position."

She stood in front of him, her hand clamped to his upper arm like a claw, her body swaying from side to side like a popsicle stick caught in a breeze. Meanwhile, the blonde on the tape moved like a supple willow tree, her fingertips resting softly on her partner's shoulder. Brady led Molly to the sofa. "Maybe we've done enough for one night."

She remained standing. "Is something wrong?"

"No. Of course not. We'll try this again another time. We've got a week before we go to Grand Pass."

"I'm ready to dance now." She went to the TV cabinet, opened a drawer and took out a CD. "But I'm tired of that lazy old music on the tape. Let's speed things up." She turned off the VHS machine and turned on the CD player. In a moment, Alan Jackson had picked up the pace with "Chattahoochee," one of the best known two-step songs ever written. She smiled sweetly at Brady, tucked her hair behind her ears and tapped the toe of her sneaker on the floor. "You ready?"

He imagined her feet stomping on his at this fast tempo but held out his hands anyway. "If you think you can do it. This song is difficult for a beginner."

She stepped close, took a deep breath and said, "Well, I'm not wearing the right shoes, but what the heck. We can give it a try."

Her perfect slim body melted into his arms like the

sweet flow of hot chocolate. Her eyes sparkled. Her hips began a slow and seductive gyration that made the blonde on the tape look like she was teaching the minuet to a bunch of Sunday-school kids. Brady gulped, held her tightly and tried to keep up. She glided across the floor.

By the end of the song, he was panting for a couple of reasons and sweating for a couple of reasons. And he'd twirled her around in steps that he hadn't known existed.

When the last guitar strain faded, she turned the volume down and looked at him with immense satisfaction. "I hope your knee's okay."

"It's fine."

Molly's hair fell in messy waves around her shoulders. Her nostrils flared slightly. Her lips gleamed as she moistened them. Flushed and energized and too damn sexy for words, she said, "How'd I do?"

He blew out a breath and struggled to catch the next one. "You cheat," he finally managed to say.

"Don't be silly. You're just a good teacher."

"Nobody's that good. And besides, in this case, you taught me plenty—never to trust you again, for one."

She picked up a Coke and took a long swig. He couldn't take his eyes off her lips pressed against the opening of the bottle. He stared at her neck, head tilted back. And then she wiped her mouth with the back of her hand and laughed. He'd never heard her really laugh before. "Surprised you, did I?"

"You sneaky woman."

She handed him the Coke after she'd had a drink, a natural, intimate gesture that completely unnerved him. He put his mouth where hers had been.

"For heaven's sake, Brady," she said. "I'm from Texas just like you are." She looked around the well-furnished apartment and smiled. "Well, maybe not exactly like you are. My father didn't allow dancing, but I was definitely sneaky when I was a teenager. I learned. And besides I was married to a—"

She stopped. "Married to a what?" he prompted after a moment.

She looked away. "Nothing."

He took hold of her arvm, forcing her to return his gaze. "Yes, you were. You were about to tell me something about your ex-husband."

She waved her hand in front of her face as if she were chasing off a pesky fly. "Nothing important. Just that he liked to dance."

"You're not going to get away with that crumb of information," Brady said. "I want to know about him. What did he do for a living?"

She frowned. "He worked."

Brady waited. She took the pop from him and drank.

"Oh, he worked, did he?" Brady repeated. "That tells me a lot. The guy's a dancer and a worker. What sort of work?"

"This and that."

"Mystery man, huh? Did he change into a hero costume and save entire cities?"

She gave him a cocky sort of smile. “You guessed it.”

A troubling thought suddenly occurred to him and his grin faded. “What a minute. I just called him your *ex*-husband. Is he? Or are you still married to him?”

“No, I’m not still married. He’s out of my life.”

He couldn’t hide his relief. “Then why won’t you talk about him? Was he a jerk?” Brady secretly hoped he was.

“No, he was the kind of guy everybody liked, but he’s gone now.”

“He ran off?”

“Yeah, he ran off.”

“Sorry.”

She angled her head to the side and narrowed her eyes. “I’ll bet you are.”

“Okay, you’re right. I’m not. But your ex isn’t the biggest mystery around here. You are. It’s been more than two weeks and I don’t know anything about you.”

“You know all you need to. Enough for us to see this bet to its conclusion.”

“Okay, that’s probably true. I’ve learned that you’re bright, a concerned mother, ambitious enough to accept this arrangement so you can open a shop. And tonight I found out you’re a sneaky cheat. Now, what else is there? Because I’ve decided those things aren’t enough.” He came toward her. “Tell me more.”

She backed up until she collided with the table. “Brady, we don’t have that kind of relationship.”

“The sharing kind?”

"Right. We're business partners."

Her cheeks flushed. She tried to skirt around him, but he blocked her by placing his hand on the table. He lowered his face to hers, breathed in the scent of her hair. His senses went a little crazy and he knew he was going to kiss her this time. "A lot of people start out as one kind of partner and end up as another kind."

"But not us." Her voice trembled. She might never admit it, but she wanted him to kiss her just as much as he wanted to.

"Why not us?"

"Like you said, we hardly know each other...."

He placed his hands on her temples. His thumbs caressed her cheekbones. "Molly, I'm thinking that right now I'm going to get to know you a whole lot better."

Her eyes widened. She exhaled a tremulous breath. "You can't kiss me."

"Oh, honey, I can." He lowered his mouth to hers. She bent away from him, a weak effort at resistance that was soon lost in the willing compliance of her body. When a soft moan rumbled up from her throat, he probed the line of her mouth with his tongue and she opened to him. Her mouth was warm and soft and just a bit cola sweet and he explored every inch of it. When he encircled her in his arms, she pushed at his chest, but only for a second. Her body slackened and she reached up and clasped her hands around his neck. He pulled her closer. Their bodies blended like the stringed harmony of the country waltz in the background.

He snaked his hand under her top, moving up the subtle ridges of her backbone. He curled his fingers over her shoulder. She pressed her firm breasts against his chest and the kiss became wild and desperate. Only when they were both breathless did he pull away, but not far. He wasn't ready to let her go, to be the one to separate. Their breaths mingled, damp on his lips. He traced his tongue over the bow of her upper lip, nipped at the swollen flesh.

She stopped him by pressing a finger over her mouth. When she spoke, her voice was hoarse. "I should be asking you for an apology."

He almost laughed, but instead bent his head and nuzzled her neck. "I'm always apologizing to you, but hell, I'm not going to now. I'm not the least bit sorry about what just happened. And I don't think you are, either."

She stood straight. "You can't speak for me."

"Then take this as the voice of experience," he breathed into her ear. "A girl who kisses back like you just did isn't looking for an apology."

"I did not kiss you back."

He stepped away and smiled down at her. "Funny. You and I must be talking about two different kisses." He reached for his jacket. "You're an awful good dancer, Molly. But I'm not going to be thinking about the two-step when I leave here." He opened the door. "Suddenly it's all about the kissin'."

CHAPTER TWELVE

MOLLY LEANED AGAINST THE DOOR after Brady had closed it and listened to his footsteps as he descended the stairs. She touched her lips and shivered in the cold air coming through the crack around the frame.

Shutting down the CD player she silenced Alan Jackson. "Dancing. That's what started this." It had been so long since a man had touched her.

She stood in the middle of the living room, looking around at the furnishings that had become so familiar in such a short time. Brady was everywhere in the room, filling up every inch of the space. She still felt his arms around her, his lips on hers. She rubbed her arms briskly and tried to erase Brady's face by substituting it with Kevin's, but all she saw was Brady.

Pulling the poker book out from under a stack of magazines on the coffee table where she'd hidden it, she sat on the sofa and kicked off her sneakers. She opened the book and stared at the pages before closing her eyes and leaning her head against the back of the sofa. At the moment she couldn't even be certain that a straight beat a full house.

"I'M GOING DOWN, MOM," Sam called from the living room. "Brady's out there already."

"Okay. Be careful. Don't go in the stalls."

"I know. You don't have to worry." The door slammed. Footsteps pounded on the stairs. Molly hadn't seen her son this excited on a Saturday morning in, well, ever.

She finished dressing, poured another cup of coffee and tucked her grocery list in her jeans. She and Angela were going into town to do the shopping. Angela had begun to enjoy mornings again, now that she didn't have to face the sun with a hangover.

Molly went outside and found Sam scrubbing feed buckets. When she didn't see Brady, she experienced a range of uncomfortable emotions, the biggest one being disappointment. Staying far enough away to keep water from soaking her jeans, she approached the spigot. "You coming into town with Mrs. Carrick and me?"

Sam didn't seem to notice that his own pants were wet. "Serafina said she'd show me how to make tacos," he said. "So I'll probably hang around here."

"I'll let her know I won't be here for a couple of hours. If it's okay with her, you can stay. But put on dry clothes before you go."

"I will."

She turned to go over to the house and work on

the books until Angela was ready. But Brady appeared at the breezeway opening when she walked by and she forgot all about double-entry bookkeeping. He took his hat off and grinned. "Morning."

"Hi." She resumed walking.

He took her by the arm and pulled her into the shadows. "You still ticked off at me?"

Her senses spiraled. He smelled of pine shavings with a hint of leather. Masculine. Sexy. *Stop it, Mol.* "Yes."

"You still want an apology?"

"Yes."

"Haven't you forgiven me just a little?"

I haven't forgiven and certainly haven't forgotten. "No."

"Do you want to do it again?"

It's all I can think about. "How can you even ask me that?"

"Because I think maybe you do."

Molly stared at the mischievous twinkle in his eyes and knew she was losing control of this conversation. She couldn't let that happen. Most of all, she couldn't admit that he was right. Ignoring the jitters that had just attacked her stomach, she said, "This arrangement between us is supposed to be purely business."

He smiled. "And that's the way you want it?"

"Yes. I want to win in Vegas. From the beginning it's what I've wanted, why I'm here."

"To open a shop?" The skepticism in his voice stung.

"Yes, that's right."

"Okay, but all work and no play…"

"Will help me win," she finished for him.

"Look, Molly, I'm going to teach you to win, but I've got a problem you can help me with."

"What are you talking about?"

"You know my friend Blake, the one who lives in San Antonio?"

"Sure. I met him at the party."

"Right. You met his wife, too. Annie works for the River Bluff newspaper. Anyway, for some reason she's set her matchmaking sights on me."

"I don't understand."

"I agreed to go on a blind date with a friend of Annie's tonight."

"Good for you. Have fun." Her words were as flat and cold as she suddenly felt.

"I don't want to go. I want to stay right here and play poker with you, and dance again, and maybe one thing will lead to another…."

She wrenched her arm free of his grasp. "Go on your date, Brady. You can't disappoint a friend. We can play poker on Sunday."

"I'd rather take you on the date."

"You and I don't date. I don't date at all. You know that. I've got Sam."

His expression turned thoughtful as he studied her. "Here's an observation. You use Sam as a means of keeping us apart an awful lot."

"That's ridiculous. There is no *together* for you and me. There's only apart."

"That's not what I felt last night."

"Forget last night. It shouldn't have happened. It won't happen again."

He raised his eyebrows. "You wanna bet?"

"Yeah, on poker. Nothing else. I thought this wager meant something to you. When you want to get serious about teaching me the game again, you come on up. I'll be ready."

"That's the way you want me to be? Serious only about poker?"

"Yes, of course."

He looked down, shook his head. "Fine. I've got a horse over there in the pasture that keeps me damn serious about this tournament, so I can play this straight." When he raised his face, his expression was distant. "Sunday, Monday and Tuesday nights. I'll be about as serious as a Texas cyclone."

"Good. That's the way I want it."

He settled his hat on his head and turned toward the breezeway. "We're still going to Grand Pass next Saturday morning."

"I'm okay with that. It's business and I need the practice."

He made a sound like a growl. "It's a good thing Wednesday night is my poker night with the guys. I think all this card-playing sobriety between you and me is going to drive me a little nuts."

She watched him walk away. *You're not going to be half as crazy as I will be thinking of you on that blind date.*

AT FIVE-THIRTY on Wednesday Brady came into the house. He'd just left the stables where he'd spent the day with Bob Holiday, the River Bluff vet. Anxious to get showered and dressed for the poker game, he strode down the hallway to the stairs leading to his room on the second floor. At his father's office he stopped and looked inside. Marshall was behind his desk watching a video of one of the horses. "Hey, Dad."

Marshall turned off the TV. "Hi, son."

"You playing tonight?"

"No. Dobbs is still in Austin visiting his girls."

"That doesn't matter," Brady said. "You can ride with me."

"Thanks, but I'm tuckered out. I don't have the stamina of you younger bucks. I'll probably just put my feet up and watch television with about two fingers of bourbon in a tumbler."

Brady smiled. "Right. You don't have the stamina. Who was that cowboy I saw on the track today riding Briar's Companion? He looked a lot like you."

Marshall chuckled. "But I kept him to a gallop. That two-year-old has to be ready for the spring racing season at Retama. I tested him out in a few quarter-miles."

"He looks good."

"I want you to breeze him, son. I've got twenty pounds on you, too heavy to put him through anything faster than a gallop. And you need to work with him on fast-footed breaks so he's ready for the starting gate. And gradually work him into furlongs. I want to see him beat forty-two seconds."

"I can do that."

Marshall nodded. "How's the bet coming with Molly?"

Brady didn't see any reason to tell his father that the past three nights of intensive poker study with Molly had left him feeling as tightly wound as a wet lariat. The all-business promise was going to damn near kill him. "I figured her for a quick study and
she hasn't disappointed me. She may not win at the quarter finals but she'll put up a good show."

"I like your confidence, son. I'll bet you're already scheduling training sessions with Amber Mac."

"I've got him used to the bit. Dobbs said it was time. And I've set up a tentative plan for introducing him to weight and saddle-breaking."

Marshall smiled affectionately, almost like he used to when Brady's accomplishments on the football field made him proud. "Looks like this deal with Molly is just a formality," he said. "As far as Mac's concerned, anyway."

"A bet's a bet, Dad. I'm not expecting any concessions from you. Besides, you know what's really at stake here."

Marshall leaned back in his chair. "Is that all you want when this bet is over, Dobbs's job?"

"What do you mean?"

"I'm just wondering. Anything else going on between you and Molly other than cards?"

That was the question that kept Brady awake at nights. That and reliving those few red-hot kisses. "No. Just poker."

"She's a cute gal…"

Marshall stopped talking and his attention shifted to the office door. Brady followed his gaze and saw Angela, cheerfully dressed in a checkered blouse and tight-fitting jeans. Her hair was pulled back into a clip at her neck and her cheeks glowed a healthy pink.

"Hi, Mom," Brady said.

"Hello, honey. You playing poker tonight?"

"Yep."

She smiled at Marshall. "Dinner will be ready in a few minutes," she said. "We can still make the eight o'clock movie in New Braunfels."

Marshall looked at Brady and cleared his throat. "That's fine, Angela."

"You haven't changed your mind, have you?" she asked.

"No, no. I'm looking forward to it."

She waved and breezed off down the hallway.

Brady scratched the back of his neck. "Tuckered out, eh? Putting your feet up and watching TV?"

Marshall frowned. "You don't have to know everything that goes on around here, Brady. Suffice it to say, there is life beyond poker and racehorses."

Brady grinned, headed to the door. "I'll try to remember that."

BRADY TURNED onto Cypress Loop Road well before the poker game was to start. Only Jake's cycle was parked in the lot. Brady exhaled a sigh of relief as he walked around to the front of the bar that faced the Medina River and a grove of Cypress trees. He wanted a few minutes of solitude in this familiar setting to contemplate the changes going on in his life.

He mounted the front porch, like countless cowboys and gamblers before him, for a breath of fresh air. Leaning against one of the ragged railings, something stung his palm. A splinter. He carefully pulled it out of the base of his thumb.

The members of the once infamous Wild Bunch had helped Jake clean up the back apartment in the bar when he returned to River Bluff a few weeks ago. Having forgiven Jake for abruptly leaving River Bluff years ago, Cole was supervising the construction job. Jake's unexpected decision to hire Rachel to renovate the inside had brought them close, and now they were making plans to build a house together on the property. Brady smiled to himself. He thought he knew these guys like they were family, yet each of them continued to surprise him with their choices.

He breathed in the smell of the river and the rich, fertile earth. The only sounds were the rustle of the wind in the trees and those cicadas that hadn't burrowed in for the long, cool night. As so often happened in his quiet moments, Brady's thoughts immediately turned to that night in Vegas when everything changed.

After three hours of play, Kevin had run out of money. As his alcohol consumption had increased, so had his belligerence. He'd made veiled threats and blatant accusations. Brady wished the cowboy had taken his advice in the bar at the Mirage and gone away with his bull-riding winnings intact.

"Lend me some money. I'm good for it," he'd practically begged. He'd unbuckled his watch and flung it on the table claiming it was a trophy from some rodeo in Dallas three years earlier. To guys who wore gold Rolexes, the steel-cased Seiko wasn't much of an ante.

"You're done, fella," one of the men had said. "Go home and sleep it off."

He'd stood up and, with one hand, raked the chips from the center of the table, scattering them on the floor. When he'd threatened to upend the table, Les had had enough. "Get out of here on your own two legs or we'll throw you out."

Brady had coaxed the trembling man to the door and taken three one-hundred-dollar bills from his wallet. He folded them and stuck them in the cowboy's pocket. "This should get you home, buddy," he'd said. "Go back to wherever you came from. You'll recover from this loss in time."

But, once again, the advice was lost on a man who wasn't ready to hear it. The last Brady saw of the cowboy, he was stumbling down the hallway.

Twenty minutes later, they'd heard the sirens. Out the window, they could see that the police had surrounded a body sprawled on the pavement. The medical personnel weren't hurrying, so it was obvious they were dealing with a dead person.

The probe into the cowboy's death was quick and conclusive. The whole incident had been caught on a surveillance camera mounted to the roof of the building. Alone and without apparent provocation, the man had climbed onto the concrete wall bordering the roof, looked down for a few seconds and plunged headfirst in an awkward swan dive. Brady left town for good a few hours after the incident and headed back to River Bluff.

The media had been vague in reporting the story. No names but the cowboy's had been included in the brief paragraph in the next day's paper.

"If I'd only..." Brady mumbled the words he'd said countless times since that night. If I'd only talked him out of coming. If I'd only made him leave sooner. If I'd only refused to let him in....

Brady shook his head and stared through the oak and cypress trees. This winding river and the Wild Card had been the scenes of some of the most memorable moments of his life, good and bad. "After all this time," he said, "why can't I stop thinking about that cowboy?"

"What are you muttering about now?"

Brady spun around at the familiar voice. He hadn't heard Jake come onto the porch. "Same old stuff," he said.

Jake put his hand on Brady's shoulder. "Let it go, B.C. There's a word for what's troubling you. *History.* That means it's in the past. You can't change it and, in this case, you didn't cause it."

The guys in River Bluff, the ones he truly called his friends, knew what happened that night in Vegas. He'd finally told Jake, the last to hear, when he was working one night at the Wild Card, making the apartment livable. Cole and Jake had stopped scraping and just sat in the middle of the freshly stripped floor, popped the tabs off some beers and listened to the story.

Though Brady had come clean to his friends, he hadn't told his family and the folks at Cross Fox. His parents believed him when he said he lost a lot of money gambling and came home to think about the direction he wanted his life to take. Brady frowned. It was true, only missing some details—ones Brady would carry in his conscience forever.

Jake stuck his hand in his pocket, probably fingering that old stone from the river he kept as some sort of talisman, ironically linking him to a past he claimed he didn't want to remember. It wasn't so long ago that he said he didn't want anything to do with the Wild Card Saloon, either, which his uncle Verne had taken care of for him. And a fine job Verne had done. Right. Now Jake was fixing the place up and even planning a future in River Bluff now that he hooked up with Rachel again. "You're not going to get all maudlin on us tonight, are you?" Jake said.

"Nope, going to try not to, anyway."

Jake gave him a half smile. "It's all history, B.C., all of it. Now, let's just play some cards."

"You're on. And I'm planning to compete with you for life of the party."

Headlights drew both men's attention to the road. "That looks like Luke pulling in," Jake said, going into the bar.

Brady followed him. "Let the game begin."

"ARE YOU GUYS going to talk about women the whole night?" Knut tossed his small blind bet into the center of the table and stared at the other eight men. "Because if you are, somebody should order the pizza. Maybe the sound of my own chewing will block out your voices."

Cole laughed. "You have a fight with Sally again, Knut?"

"No, but all this talk about the fairer sex is enough to make me go back and start one."

Luke raised the dog tags from his hole cards and peeked at them one more time before calling the bet to see the flop. "You don't hear me talking about women," he said.

"Yeah, but you're thinking about one," Jake said.

Ed Falconetti nodded. "Right. What's going on between you and Becky Howard, anyway?"

Luke tugged his hat down low on his brow and slouched in his chair. "Nothing's going on. Why would you ask that?"

"I hear things at the café. You've run into her a couple of times."

"It's a small town, Ed. Of course I've run into her."

Ron Hayward, Cole's former construction boss

called the bet. Ron only played with them occasionally. Some of the other guys didn't like him much, but Brady was always glad to see him at the table. He had money and bet loosely. "Becky's cute," Ron said.

All the guys stared at him as if he'd just said martians had landed by the Medina river. He never talked about much that wasn't game-related. When he realized he was the center of attention, his face reddened. "What? She is cute."

Blake laughed. "So's that lady living out at Cross Fox," he said. "Anything happening between you two yet?" he asked Brady.

Brady shuddered at this question. Of all the guys, Blake was the one he least wanted to lie to. Since Cole introduced them, Brady had always thought of Blake as a true go-to guy. "No. Just business," he said. That's the way Molly would have answered the question; it wasn't really a lie.

"Fine by me," Blake said, flashing a half smile. "So what'd you think of that woman Annie fixed you up with the other night?"

Blake had provided the perfect opportunity for Brady to steer the conversation away from him and Molly. "She was all right. I might see her again."

Blake raised the bet. "Can I tell Annie that? She's asked me a couple of times."

Brady called the raise. "No, you'd better not."

"Didn't think so."

The dealer rolled over the flop. Brady felt a small vibration travel across a floorboard under the table. Ron was tapping his foot, a sure sign he had a hand.

"I'm all-in," Ron said when the betting came around to him again. Brady figured he had a third jack in his hand to match the two on the table, and he folded. Only Jake stayed in and ultimately lost with his ace high. That was okay. Jake would win some hands before the night was over.

"So how's that bet going?" Ed asked when Jake went to the phone to order pizza.

Brady gave his usual weekly update, detailing Molly's progress. He couldn't go anywhere in town anymore without somebody bringing up the now infamous wager.

"You know there's been a chart of side bets hanging in the café for over a week now. Folks are wagering on whether Molly will get to the final table."

"Yeah? Do the odds keep changing? They should because she's getting better every day."

Ed chuckled. "I'd still like to talk to her about working for me."

Brady kept his cool. "She's doing fine where she is," he said. "But you do what you want."

"Maybe I will."

Jake returned to the table, wiggled his fingers. "Pony up, guys. Five bucks each for pizza."

Cole tossed his five across the table. "I've been thinking…"

Luke fished five dollars out of his wallet. "There's a news flash."

"No, really." He studied Brady. "When is the tournament?"

"Begins Friday, February 22nd."

"A little over two weeks from now." Cole looked over at the old Wild Bunch. "I'm free that weekend."

Jake stuffed the cash into his shirt pocket. "And that's supposed to affect my life how?"

Cole stuck his arms out like the wings of an airplane and made engine noises.

The table was silent for a minute until Jake smiled. "Hell, count me in."

"I'm pretty sure Annie and I can be there," Blake said.

"Tessa would love to see Sin City again," Cole said. "It wasn't so long ago we were all there for Blake's wedding, so why not be there for Brady and his gal?"

"She's not my gal," Brady said.

Blake smiled. "Right. She's your business partner. So who wants to make the reservations?"

CHAPTER THIRTEEN

MOLLY SAT FORWARD, tugging against the pickup's seat belt. "Did I hear you correctly? Your buddies are coming to Vegas for the quarter finals?"

He'd waited to tell her that minor detail until they were an hour away from River Bluff. He didn't want her getting spooked about the possibility of an audience. She might call the whole thing off and order him to turn around and head back to the ranch. "That's what they said."

"And you think they're serious?"

He shrugged. "I have to, especially when money's involved. Blake hired a private jet to take us all and each guy chipped in part of the cost. Looks like River Bluff, Texas, will be well represented." He paused before adding, "Might be a few others besides my poker buddies, as well." He gave her a smile he hoped would put her at ease. "That doesn't bother you, does it?"

"Having your friends at the tournament, evaluating my decisions, drawing conclusions about my intelligence—or lack of? No, why should that bother me?"

He laughed. "They'll be judging me a whole lot more than they'll judge you. I'm the one who swore I could lead you to the final table."

She stared out the window at the flat prairie that had spread endlessly in front of them ever since they'd left the hill country. A ten o'clock sun burnished the spines of cacti and rugged yuccas. "I sure hope you know what you're doing, then."

He took his eyes off the road long enough to notice the delicate wrinkle between her brows, the slight downturn of her full lips. Her worry stirred something instinctive and protective inside him. All he wanted was to kiss that pout until he made her forget about the tournament. Instead, he refocused on the asphalt. "I do."

She clenched her hands in her lap. "What is this trip today going to cost you? Just the fifty-dollar entrance fee?"

"That's it. Unless you want to play two tournaments. And I don't plan on losing the fifty. I expect you'll do very well and we'll split the winnings. But if you want to get technical, I suppose it'll cost me the price of your lunch, too."

"Don't worry about that. I can't eat a bite."

"You'll be surprised how much winning can increase the appetite."

"I don't think so in my case." She squinted into the sun. "How much farther?"

"About another twenty-five miles. That's around-the-corner in Texas-speak. And plenty of time for a refresher course in tournament play."

"Okay. That's a good idea. Give me some last-minute pointers."

"How about true or false questions? You ready?"

"Shoot."

"Question number one. True or false. To start, there will be ten people at the table, nine players and a dealer."

"Easy. True."

He faked a chalk line in the air with his finger to indicate she was correct. "Two. If a player verbally announces a raise, but only slides in a fraction of that amount to the pot, it's the actual number of chips that count."

She chewed the inside of her cheek. "True?"

"Oh, sweetheart, no. That's false. Moral: always be careful what you say. Which brings to mind question number three. It's okay to talk about the hands as they're being played."

"I know this one. It's never all right to talk about that."

Brady smiled, recalling the night Luke talked too much and ended up wearing Knut's hamburger. "Even if you're not in the hand?" he asked. "Can you talk about the cards then?"

"Nope."

"Right you are. But how about this? It's okay to bat your eyelashes at any other player."

She frowned. "Stupid question, but I suppose it's true."

"Damn straight and I suggest you do it. In your case, it will be an essential part of your strategy. Next question, in a no-limit game, the amount of the raises in any betting round is unlimited."

"That's how no-limit got its name."

"Correct. Last question for now. After the tournament, win or lose, you absolutely, positively must two-step with me in the casino dance hall."

He waited a beat. "You're taking too long to answer. That kind of careful consideration is okay at the poker table, but not when my pride is at stake." He pretended to scowl while pointing to the backseat of the truck. "I've been practicing, lady, and I've got a brand-new pair of boots in a box back there that are just your size."

She looked over the seat. "How'd you know my size?"

"I have a spy in your apartment." Brady held his hand to the height of the truck roof. "A guy about this tall. He brought me one of your sneakers when he got home from school yesterday."

Her mouth lifted in the hint of a smile. "Okay then. But those boots had better not pinch my feet."

FOUR HOURS LATER Brady led Molly into the Grand Pass Casino buffet. "You must be starved," he said, his own mouth watering at the tempting horseshoe-shaped display of Mexican and Southwestern foods. "That bagel sandwich you had before the first tournament must have worn off a long time ago."

She raised her eyebrows and pointed to her stomach. "Wrong. It's still sitting here like a lead weight."

He picked up a tray and handed it to her. "That'll pass. First-timer jitters, that's all it is."

She slid her tray mechanically along the stainless rail while he piled food on his. "I think you could eat anytime," she observed, "even if you were playing for a thousand dollars a hand."

"Yeah, you're right. I've had a love affair with food all my life." He stared at her tray where she'd just placed a small taco salad. "You can do better than that."

"I'm still looking," she said. "I'd probably be hungrier if I'd played better."

He reached for a piece of key lime pie. "What are you talking about? You did great."

"Sure. First one out in the first tournament."

He conceded with a nod. "That could happen to anyone. You had a pair of aces, and another turned up on the flop. You went all-in, just as you should have. By all rights, you should have won the pot."

She flinched. "Too bad about that guy pulling a straight."

"It happens," Brady said. "He had the ten and queen in the hole, and a nine, jack, king came on the flop. That's what we call a bad beat, Molly. Just rotten luck. And it's not likely to ever happen to you again in your short but hopefully illustrious poker career." He smiled, satisfied to see her add a cheese enchilada to her tray. "Besides, look how you did in the second tournament."

"Third isn't winning."

"No, but third is darned good for a beginner. You played right and that's what I wanted to see. And we're splitting a hundred and fifty bucks." He pulled the cash from his shirt pocket while they waited at the cash register to pay.

"Keep the amount you paid for the entrance fee and we'll split the rest," she said.

"No way. I said we'd go fifty-fifty on the winnings and that's what we're doing." He counted out seventy-five dollars, folded it and stuffed it in her jeans pocket. "How's that feel?" he asked.

"An extra seventy-five bucks feels darned good, I must admit."

"Not the money," he said. "I was wondering how it felt when I put my hand in your pocket."

A spurt of laughter escaped her, but she quickly stifled it. "You're impossible."

"Maybe, but I've become the best two-stepper in south central Texas, so eat up." He checked his watch. "According to my schedule, we've got about an hour to kill on the dance floor before we head back to River Bluff."

She walked to an empty table. "We should be home by dark, then."

He pulled a chair out for her. "Don't count on it. I've got seventy-five dollars in my pocket." He looked around the restaurant where most of the clientele was middle-aged or older. "And none of these other women seem interested in me."

MOLLY DECIDED that Brady had been telling the truth about practicing his steps, though she sensed he was paying for his new moves with a few extra twinges in his knee. He claimed the attention they'd gotten on the dance floor had to do with Molly's presence at the poker tables earlier. He insisted that some of her opponents had wandered into the ballroom and had been as focused on her dancing as they'd been on her game. He referred to her special talent at the tables as the eyelash-batting technique.

She should have let him know that his conclusion was slightly degrading, that she'd impressed the other players with her skills, not her looks, but what the heck? It was nice to simply bask in masculine praise once in a while, even though she knew, deep down, that Brady didn't mean it. She'd always thought of herself as okay-looking, but mostly plain. She'd never had the money or opportunity to buy the accessories other women used to improve on nature's flaws.

And of course, her father would have pitched a fit if he'd seen her face covered in makeup. Kevin wouldn't have liked it, either. The big-haired, painted women who followed the rodeo circuit never interested him. After a few weeks on the tour, he was glad to come home to his Mol, the prettiest girl in Prairie Bend. Knowing that the town only had a population of fifteen hundred, and most of the women her age had married young and had a flock of kids, Molly hadn't let it go to her head.

In the casino parking lot, Brady opened the truck door and waited for her to climb in. As he walked around to the driver's side, she thought about his behavior toward her today and decided it wasn't so different from the attention he gave Amber Mac. He treated the prize horse with special deference, seeing that he was well fed, praised and shoed. She looked down at her new boots and smiled. *Looks like Brady expects a lot from both of us.*

He got in the truck and started the engine. "Hope all that dancing helped you work off that pitiful lunch," he said.

Relaxed and even feeling lazy after the tension of the tournaments and the energy of the two-step, she laid her head back. "When we get back to Cross Fox, I could eat."

"Good, but we're not going to Cross Fox. Not right away."

She swiveled her head to look at his profile. "We're not?"

"No. We're going to San Antonio for dinner first."

She sat forward. "I can't do that. There's Sam—"

"I told you, Dobbs and Serafina are taking him to a movie tonight and after that…" He stopped. "If you don't believe me, get out your cell phone and call. Make sure everything's okay."

She did. Sam got on the line and chattered for several minutes about the fun he'd had and the movie he was going to see. Next, Serafina put Molly at ease, telling her that she and Dobbs were the ones enjoying themselves. After Molly disconnected, she looked at Brady who was pushing the truck at a smooth eighty miles an hour over the open road. "It should be okay if you want to go to dinner."

Two hours later, the sun had set and Brady pulled in front of a restaurant hidden behind a heavy iron fence. Twinkling white lights winked from a wall of flowers. A uniformed valet opened the door for Molly. She glanced over at Brady. "I don't think seventy-five dollars is going to cover dinner for two at this place."

He smiled. "Don't worry—this is my treat. I'm only having soup and water."

She noticed the word *steakhouse* on the wooden placard mounted to the ornately scrolled gate. "A Texan having soup in a place like this? I don't think so."

THE FIVE-OUNCE FILET cooked to medium-well perfection was delicious. Normally Molly didn't eat red meat. It wasn't a life choice. It was more an economical one, but she enjoyed the entire dinner, including two glasses of merlot and crème brûlée for dessert.

Brady held her elbow as they left the restaurant. He took her across the street to a park with an inviting gazebo in the center. "Are you cold?" he asked, turning the collar up on her jacket.

"No. This walk is just what I need after eating such a big meal." She studied a nearby building with fanciful turn-of-the-century cast-iron lights outside. Green awnings shaded the windows of the top stories and ornate grillwork protected French doors topped with fan windows. "The Menger Hotel," Molly said, reading the name under the third-floor cornice. "I've heard of this."

"It's a San Antonio landmark," Brady said. "Cattlemen have stayed here for decades. Still do when they prefer tradition over the more modern hotels on the River Walk."

They cleared a stand of trees in the park and came face-to-face with a rustic stone building. "Oh, my gosh," Molly said. "That's the Alamo."

"Sure is."

"Right here in the center of town. I've never seen it. It's very impressive with the lights shining on it."

The doors on the old mission were closed and locked, but Brady walked her up close. "What do you think of it?"

"I'm awestruck," she said.

"Smaller than you'd imagined?"

"It's so…humble…makes the efforts of those outnumbered men even more impressive."

"The mission compound was much larger in the early 1800s," Brady explained. "The city forced preservationists to give up some of the acreage."

They proceeded down a walkway protected by a stone wall bordering the Alamo property and passed a security guard who smiled and wished them a good evening. Then they strolled leisurely beyond the wall to where the sidewalk led through live oak trees and evergreen shrubs. Streetlights were limited in this area, and they were soon in shadows. Brady stopped walking, wrapped his hand around Molly's arm and turned her to face him. In spite of the chill in the air, a burst of heat warmed her face. He was so close, his face only inches from hers.

He smiled down at her. "I was beginning to wonder if we'd find a quiet moment together this whole day."

She swallowed. "A quiet moment for what?"

Gently, he tugged her closer. "You know, for a smart woman, Molly, you can be…"

She pressed her palm on his chest. "Brady, you've been a perfect gentleman all day."

"Yeah, and it's been killing me. It's not that I mind the perfect part. It's the *gentleman* part I'm having trouble with."

All her senses went on alert. His soft gaze became magnified in her perception. His woodsy scent mingled with the trees around them. For this moment she wanted to ignore her conscience and just feel his chest against hers and their hearts beating together. She wanted to forget that he was the man who stole her life.

"I'm tired of these stupid rules between us," he said. "I don't want to be good anymore. What's the harm if we give in to our feelings?"

What's the harm? The innocent enormity of his question brought her back to reality. "We can't, Brady. It's wrong."

He cupped her chin. "We can and it's not. Kissing you feels about as right as anything I've ever done."

She should have looked away, down at the sidewalk, up at the sky, anywhere but his eyes. But she didn't. She looked directly at him as if she were immune to his effect which, of course, she wasn't. She was trapped in a moment from which there was no escape. He tipped her chin up, lowered his mouth and kissed her deeply. And she let him. Worse, she encouraged him. She parted her lips and let him in. *Sweet heaven,* she thought.

He'd discovered the undeniable truth. She wanted him every bit as much as he claimed he wanted her.

The air around them was cold and dry. Yet his hands on each side of her face were warm and comforting in their urgency to hold her close. His body heat spread to her limbs and made her weak. She leaned against him, relishing the feel of him. Everywhere they touched, there was that incredible, penetrating warmth.

He slipped his hand inside her jacket and cupped her breast over her blouse. The tip pebbled instantly, and he massaged it with his thumb. She took a quick breath. Her chest rose to meet his hand. He backed her against a tree and slid his leg between hers. His thigh rubbed against her, sending a delicious pressure through her panties and making her dizzy. She reached around his neck and clung to him, caught between the hardness of the tree and the solid expanse of his chest. He nuzzled her neck as he slipped the buttons on her blouse free. His hand worked under the lace of her bra. "I want you, Molly." He breathed into her ear. "We don't have to be back tonight."

She fought for logical thought through the haze of her desire. "But we do. Sam…"

"Serafina knows we might be late. I asked her if Sam could stay over."

She was light-headed, almost giddy. "Oh. That was…"

He nipped at her earlobe. "Pure genius?"

She arched her neck to give him access to every inch of her throat.

His voice husky, he said, "The Menger. It's only three blocks. Say you'll stay there with me." With a groan, he tugged the lapels of her jacket closed and kissed her. "Say you'll stay, Molly."

Her breath came in ragged gasps. She wanted to say yes but the words wouldn't come. Somewhere in the back of her mind she knew she should say no. But those words were even more lost, so he took her silence to mean the answer he wanted.

He put his arm around her and led her toward the hotel. They passed the security guard, this time without speaking. They crossed the street and entered the lobby. Molly stood at the side while Brady went to the front desk. He spoke to the clerk and handed over his credit card. The guy must have said something funny, because Brady chuckled, at ease with what was about to happen. And instantly Molly realized that she wasn't.

Common sense subdued the crazy rush of emotions she'd been feeling, perhaps because of the strict evangelical principles she'd warred with her entire life. But mostly because she knew this was wrong. "Brady." He put up one finger, smiled. But she persisted and pulled him away from the desk.

She forced her heartbeat to return to normal, looked up at Brady and said, "Take me back to Cross Fox."

CHAPTER FOURTEEN

BRADY STARED AT HER. "What? You want to go home?"

"That's what I said."

Her features were resolute, her voice calm, in control. And Brady knew he wasn't going to undress Molly tonight unless it was in his imagination. And he'd already done that dozens of times. "I thought you wanted..."

"What you want? Maybe I did, for a minute. But not after I've had a chance to think. Please get your truck."

His brain buzzed with the sudden one-eighty as he walked back to the restaurant. Pulling in front of the hotel, he blew out a long breath as he waited for her to get in. This was all his fault, damn it. He'd been encouraging Molly to think since the day she arrived at Cross Fox. Now he just wanted her to *feel.* He raised his eyes to the tree-lined pathway that wound away from the Alamo. "Molly, back there, on the sidewalk...didn't you...weren't you...?"

"I got carried away. You should be thankful you didn't waste money on an expensive room."

He snorted. "You and I have a completely different opinion on what constitutes wasting money. Just ten minutes ago I would have sworn we both thought a measly hotel bill was money well spent."

"I've told you before. Our relationship is business."

That same stale line was making him crazy. "Cut the bull, Molly—"

"We shouldn't cross a line that has been clear from the moment we talked in the diner parking lot in Prairie Bend."

"If you can't tell that our relationship has changed, then I've been wrong about you. Maybe all you care about is money."

She drew her trembling lips between her teeth and stared straight ahead. He knew she cared about a lot more than winning a poker tournament. Why the hell wouldn't she admit it?

He tried again. "Obviously, back there—" he pointed to the trees "—we weren't formulating our next business proposition." Brady's anger was fired by emotions that had had no release. "It's time for us to own up to this business thing you're trying to convince yourself actually exists."

"It does exist. I'm not convincing myself of anything."

She was a terrible liar.

She clenched her hands in her lap and turned to look at him. "Brady, why exactly do you want to sleep with me?"

"Why does any man want to sleep with any woman?" His voice was harsh, defensive, but so what? That's how she made him feel.

She fixed him with a stony glare. "I think you should start driving now. We must be nearly an hour away from Cross Fox."

He gave a quick look in the side mirror and stepped on the accelerator. After fifteen excruciatingly silent minutes, they were on a deserted stretch of two-lane highway that headed into the rural hill country. He'd started to calm down, but he wasn't there yet. A whole lot of anger still churned inside him. Not to mention a tightening in his groin that was stubbornly refusing to give him a break.

After a few miles, she said, "Do you mind if I turn on the radio?"

"Go ahead."

She found a country music station and adjusted the volume to a near deafening pitch. He reached over and turned it down. "What do you want me to say, Molly?"

"I don't want you to say anything. I was enjoying the music."

The hell she was. He drummed his fingers on the steering wheel. "Do you want flowers and sloppy sentiments? Do you want me to bare my soul?"

"No. I want the music back up."

"Because you're not likely to get any of that stuff. I don't gush. I don't overanalyze." He jabbed his chest with his index finger. "I just *feel,* something you obviously don't know how to do."

The look she gave him was like a slap in the face. "I just wanted to make love to a woman who seemed to want it, too." He held up his index finger. "And you know what, Molly? That's not wrong. That's normal, healthy."

Her lips set in a firm line, she wrenched the radio dial. A commercial for a place called Stockcar Heaven blared through the truck. Just as fiercely, Brady turned it off. "It's your ex-husband, isn't it?" he said. "You're making me pay the price for something that jerk did to you."

"Shut up, Brady." She folded her arms over her chest and looked out the side window. A minute later he saw her wipe her cheek. Damn. She was crying. He'd wanted her to feel something, but now that she was, he didn't have the first clue how to deal with it. He waited until he thought the silence in the car would cause blood vessels to pop in his head. Then he turned the radio back on. "Is this station still okay?"

She nodded. "It's fine. Can't you go any faster?"

He sure as hell could. And, ignoring that he'd already racked up too many speeding tickets in Bandera County, he did.

MOLLY RUBBED HER CHEEK with the sleeve of her jacket. *Just wait for that tournament, Brady. Wait till you find out who I am, what you did to my life.* She almost told him right then, but knew the moment would be sweeter when she had that prize money in her hand. Then Brady would finally understand who the real jerk was. And he'd realize that she'd been paying the price for the part he'd played in her husband's death. And her son paid, too. And most of all, Kevin. Molly wondered if Brady had ever paid a price for anything he'd done in his entire silver-spoon-fed life.

And to think that just minutes ago she'd let herself feel comforted—desired—in his arms. She'd even foolishly allowed herself to believe that he might love her. Of course he didn't love her. If he did, what a horrible mess that would be. She could never love him. A woman can't love a man she can never forgive.

She stole a glance at him. The lights from the dashboard illuminated his hands on the steering wheel. He flexed his fingers. She watched the knuckles contract and release and remembered with terrifying clarity that those skillful hands had touched her in places that had been untouched for so many long months. He'd brought her alive with his kisses and caresses. His breath had warmed her skin, fanned emotions she'd sworn she'd never experience again.

She leaned her head against the window. The glass cooled the heated skin at her temple. *Thank heavens you didn't get a room with him,* she thought. She'd been so close. Her body had responded so powerfully… *Stop it, Molly. Don't think about it.* But her breasts still tingled. Her lips still pulsed from the sweet pressure of his mouth.

There was only one way to deal with a man who

tempted her with every smile and touch. She had to beat him.

Brady turned into Cross Fox, sped up the drive to the stables and stopped in front of the stairs to the apartment. He leaned over her and opened the door. “Is this okay?” he said. “I’m not walking you up. My status as the perfect gentleman is already tarnished.”

“I’m capable of walking up by myself,” she said.

“I’m sure Sam’s already asleep over at Dobbs’s place.”

“Yes. I won’t wake him.” She started to get out but paused with one foot on the ground. “The quarter finals are less than two weeks away,” she said. “You still want to go through with this?”

He blasted her with a cold stare. “Hell, yes. It’s all about money anyway, isn’t it?”

“Yes. And speaking of that…”

His eyes narrowed. “Yeah?”

“I’ve thought of a way to increase our odds of winning.”

“You mean *your* odds?”

“No. I mean, ours. You should enter the tournament, too.”

He stared over the steering wheel. “Not part of the deal.”

“No, but is there anything really preventing you from being a player?”

“I don’t participate in serious poker anymore. It’s a promise I made myself.”

“I think you should break it, at least this one time.

That way if one of us busts out, the other might still have a chance."

"My deal with my father is that I'd coach you to the final table."

"That doesn't have to change. You'll still win the bet if I make it. You didn't stipulate that you wouldn't play, did you?"

"No, but I know how he feels about my Vegas days. And frankly, my memories of that part of my life aren't fond ones."

"I'd really like you to consider it," she said. "We'd split the winnings the same way, fifty-fifty."

A muscle worked his temple. "What brought this on?"

It was a fair question. "Now that the tournament is getting closer, I'm beginning to worry about what will happen to Sam and me if I don't make the final table. As you know, I have plans for the money."

He expelled a derisive laugh. "Oh, right. Your shop. You want me to enter so you have two chances of coming out of this with a few bucks."

"Yes. Is that unreasonable? I've invested quite a bit in this gamble, in case you've forgotten."

"Sure you have. It must have been tough to walk out on filling the coffee cups of dusty old cowboys."

She bristled at that remark, but kept her temper in check. "It was honest money. But I'm not going back there no matter what happens in Las Vegas. That's why I'd like a better chance at walking away with some cash." She stared at him, but he didn't look at her. "Will you at least give some thought to entering?" she said. "You really do owe me—more than I think you realize."

He jerked his head around and stared at her. She flinched and clamped her mouth shut before she said too much. The hard glint in his eyes warned her that perhaps she already had.

"It's late, Molly," he said. "Go on up. I'll let you know tomorrow."

She climbed up the stairs without looking back, ran into the apartment and sank down on the sofa. Her heart raced. She clutched her hands to her chest to keep them from trembling. She could do this. She could beat Brady at the same game that beat Kevin. She was good enough. Maybe then this…whatever it was she felt for Brady…would be over. She could move on. So, with a way out of this emotional quagmire a possibility, why was she still wiping tears from her eyes?

BRADY DEBATED THE WISDOM of his decision to let Luke drive him to the poker game Wednesday night when his best friend ran off the road onto the shoulder. "You're what?" Luke said.

Brady grabbed the door handle while Luke swerved back to the blacktop. "You heard me right. I'm going to enter the tournament along with Molly."

Luke shook his head. "Now I know why you asked me to drive. You're drunk."

"No, but it's not a bad idea."

"But you said you'd never play in Vegas again."

"This is different."

"How does Marshall feel about this? I know he isn't aware of what happened to that cowboy, but still, he wasn't happy when you came home broke and looking like a kicked puppy."

"I explained everything to him. Told him how Molly wanted some assurance that she'd come out of this with more than a bad taste in her mouth for me and Cross Fox Ranch. With both of us entered, she stands to walk away with some cash at least. You know Dad. He can understand why I feel responsible for her."

Luke's mouth lifted in a cocky grin. "What if she beats you?"

Brady scoffed. "She's not that good yet. But anybody can hit a lucky streak. I just hope she makes it to the final table. Hell, I hope I do, too. Then at least one of us is sure of raking in some of the big pot."

"How does this arrangement affect the original bet?"

Brady had asked his dad the same question. "Molly still has to reach the final table for me to get training rights to Amber Mac," he said. "Dad's happy with what I've done with the colt so far, but I guess I'm my father's son after all. A bet's a bet. A man's word and all that."

"Oh, yeah," Luke said, "our fathers were cut from the same cloth."

Though Marshall hadn't voiced any complaints about Brady's initial training of Amber Mac, they both understood that a bigger prize was at stake. So far Marshall hadn't said anything encouraging about his son taking over for Dobbs in a few months. And in the end, that's what Brady was working toward, that and restoring his father's confidence in him.

Luke slowed for the turn onto Cypress Loop Road. "Can I be honest with you, Brady?"

Brady smirked. "When have you ever asked my permission to be honest before?"

Luke smiled. "Back at ya' on that one. I was just thinking that maybe this poker setup has started to be about Molly."

"What? Don't be ridiculous."

Luke shrugged. "I've known you all your life, Brady, and when I see you like you're acting tonight, all tightly coiled and prickly, there's usually a woman involved."

Brady shook his head. "That's nuts."

Luke looked straight ahead. "Tomorrow's Valentine's Day. You going to send her flowers?"

"Hell, no. I don't have a valentine." If things had gone differently in San Antonio, Brady would have given Molly a whole lot more than flowers. He stared at Luke's profile. "And, just to clear the air, this bet's never been about Molly. At least not the way you're thinking. Molly was just caught in the middle."

He averted his face, choosing to stare out the window rather than allow Luke to see his features. They'd been friends for so long that even after their recent years apart, Luke could tell when he was lying and he wouldn't be shy about calling him on it.

Brady had known when he dropped Molly off on Saturday night that he would do what she wanted. When he'd gone to the apartment on Sunday to tell her he would enter the tournament, he realized that the focus of the bet had changed. Sure, Mac still meant a lot to him. The horse was his ticket into the winner's circle as a professional trainer who had every right to be there. But he didn't think of the thoroughbred as a symbol of his future anymore. Sometime in the past weeks he'd begun to think of Molly's future as somehow connected to his own. That's why, if she wanted him to enter the tournament, he would.

He didn't think he loved her exactly. How could any man love a woman who made it so damned hard? But he was close to accepting that there probably wasn't anything he wouldn't do for her. How she'd managed to make him feel this way, he didn't know, because the worst thing about their relationship was that while he'd started to see her as a part of his life, she apparently had her future all planned out and he didn't seem to be in it.

Luke parked in front of the Wild Card and cut the engine. "Hey, we're here. You still on this planet?"

Brady opened the truck door. "Let's see who's here tonight and play some cards."

Luke stepped out. "Hope you can keep your mind on the game. It's only nine days till the big event. Will your protégée be ready?"

"She'll be as ready as I can make her." He stomped up the steps to the bar. Molly could beat anybody he'd ever played with her power to concentrate on those cards. That's all she'd been doing the past few days. She was concentrating circles around him. He was the one in a tailspin.

WITH A BROOMSTICK between his legs, Sam galloped around the living-room floor in Molly's new boots, pretending to be the foreman of a cattle drive. "Are you ready for supper?" she asked him when she finally talked him into leaving his wooden horse in a corner.

"Yeah, but can I wear your boots to Las Vegas next week?"

Molly had been surprised when Brady extended an invitation to her son. At least he'd asked her permission before bringing it up to Sam, arguing that the trip was truly going to be a family affair and there would be plenty of people to watch Sam while they played.

Molly didn't have a reason to say no. If Sam didn't go, she could have left him with Becky Howard, but that didn't seem fair to her new friend. Becky had a fifteen-year-old and a full-time job. Serafina assured her that she had no real interest in poker, other than cheering for Molly and Brady, so she could send positive thoughts through the airwaves while she and Sam visited some of the sights in town. Now the trip was all Sam talked about.

"How about if I buy you a pair of boots just your size? Wouldn't that be better than wearing mine?"

He scooted ahead of her into the kitchen. "Wow, Mom, that would be really cool. Can we buy them tomorrow? Then I can wear them to school a few days before we get on the airplane." His serious expression made him seem wiser than his seven years. "A cowboy's got to break in his boots, you know. That's what Brady told me. Got to break in his boots, his hat and his horse."

"Yes, I suppose we can buy them tomorrow." She still had her winnings from Grand Pass and she couldn't think of a better way to spend the money.

He grimaced as she spooned peas onto his plate. When she added a hamburger and macaroni and cheese, he said, "That's better." He'd only eaten a few bites when he asked, "Where's Brady? He's been coming up every night getting you ready for the game. Heck, he gives you more homework than I get from Mrs. Harmon."

Molly smiled. "Brady's tough, all right. But I get a break tonight. He went to play poker with his friends."

"Oh, right. It's Wednesday." Sam scooped a spoonful of noodles into his mouth. "Maybe I can play in that game someday. When I get bigger."

"And have money of your own," she pointed out.

"Yeah, that, too."

This wasn't the first time Sam had made a reference to staying in River Bluff, and Molly figured it was time to address the issue. She set down her fork and took a sip of iced tea. "Sam, you do remember that when we came here, I told you it would only be for a short time."

He stared down at his plate. "I remember, but you also said I could pick the next place we went to."

He had a good memory. "I think I said *maybe,* and maybe you still can. I'll certainly take your choice into consideration."

He looked up at her. "River Bluff and Cross Fox is where I want to stay." He looked around the gleaming kitchen. "Heck, Mom, this is the best place we've ever lived."

She sighed. "It's nice, Sammy, I know, but Cross Fox isn't our home. We can't stay in this apartment. The Carricks have been generous to let us live here for as long as they have, but we can't impose once the tournament is over."

He thought for a moment. "You mean, we're not paying rent, don't you?"

"Well, yes, that's part of it. Most people aren't fortunate enough to live someplace completely free."

"We did at Grandpa's."

Oh, Sam, if you only knew. The price of living in her dad's house was incalculable. "Even so, honey, we have to find a place of our own, just for you and me. If I win enough money we'll find a great house or apartment every bit as nice as this one. And you can have your own room."

"Can I have a pony like Ebeneezer? And will I be able to wash the buckets and feed the big horses like Amber Mac?"

Her heart broke. "No, Sammy, probably not. But we'll discover other things that you'll like just as much."

He set down his hamburger without taking a bite.

"I don't think so, Mom. This place is great." Plopping his elbows on the table, he settled his chin in his hands. "Maybe we could stay in River Bluff, though. We don't have to stay at Cross Fox. You can open your store in town and I can come out here with you when you do the books for Serafina. That'd be okay, wouldn't it?"

If only it were that simple, but how could she tell Sam why it would never work? How could she forget Brady if she lived in River Bluff? And how could she watch him move on with his life when she wasn't a part of it? These were two questions she certainly hadn't expected to be asking herself when she packed up her stuff a few weeks ago and left Prairie Bend.

She stacked the plates and carried them to the sink. She hoped Sam wasn't waiting for an answer because she sure didn't have one. This bet was supposed to bring her peace by settling debts, giving her a better future and relieving her heartache. It wasn't supposed to create a whole new batch of problems.

SATURDAY MORNING Molly dropped Sam off at a friend's house and returned to the ranch with the intention of finishing the week's bookkeeping. She pulled up in front of the apartment just as Brady and Dobbs led Amber Mac from his stall into the open arena, one man on each side. A teenaged boy was sitting on the horse bareback. Amber Mac balked and flattened his big ears. The teen leaned low over his neck and spoke to the animal while Brady and Dobbs held him in check with taut lead lines.

Curious, Molly watched the procedure. She hesitated to approach, fearful she might spook the horse. And besides, she and Brady hadn't enjoyed the most congenial relationship since their trip to San Antonio a week ago. They had maintained a certain professionalism that should have pleased her but didn't. She sighed, observing Brady's skillful knack with the animal, his gentle but firm guidance, and hearing his calm voice as he spoke both to Amber Mac and the boy.

She turned and started up the stairs but Brady's voice stopped her on the first step. "Okay, Shane, you can dismount," he said. "Mac's had a taste of a rider, but we don't want to put too much pressure on him the first time."

Shane? Molly realized the kid on Mac's back was Becky's son. She waited as Brady watched him slide to the ground. "I think he did just fine for his first time with a rider," Shane said, patting the horse's neck. Amber Mac snorted, shaking his finely sculpted head.

"Not bad. But we have a long way to go," Brady said. He removed his lead line from Mac's bridle. "Would you cool him down?" Brady asked Dobbs.

Dobbs led Mac toward the pasture while Brady and Shane headed for the breezeway. Noticing Molly for the first time, Brady stopped. "Hey, Molly, have you ever met Becky's son?"

Shaking Shane's hand, she thought he was a handsome young man. If he had personality, as well, Becky must be having quite a time keeping the girls away. She wondered if she'd have the same worries when Sam became a teenager. She thought Sam was adorable, but of course, her impressions were colored with a mother's pride. Although not entirely. Her son had dropped a few pounds since coming to Cross Fox and he'd assumed an immeasurable amount of self-confidence. She saw a similar confidence in Shane's easy smile.

"You're my mom's new friend, aren't you?" he said.

"That's me. It's nice to finally meet you."

"Same here."

Brady laid a hand on Shane's shoulder. "Nice work. Go on to the office. I'll meet you there and pay you in a few minutes."

Shane sauntered into the breezeway. "He's a good kid," Brady said.

"Seems like it."

"He has a way of communicating with animals I haven't seen in other young men. We need that since Mac's proved he's not going to be an easy horse to train to a rider."

"I thought everything was working out with Mac," she said.

Brady's eyes sparked with enthusiasm. "He's a great horse, Molly. Don't get me wrong. His challenging spirit is good. Blake's colleague was right about him. When Mac reaches two-year-old status, he's going to set the racing world on its ear."

"I'm glad. So all I have to do is make the final table next weekend and he's all yours to train."

"That'll clinch it for sure. By the way, our tournament registrations were faxed this morning. We're both in."

She nodded, experiencing a flux of emotions between fear and excitement at the possibility of facing Brady at the final table. There was no backing out now. She only had one more week to carry the burden of her secret and then it would all be over. She would know she'd done all she could for Kevin—and for Sam and her. Then she could begin putting Brady and Cross Fox Ranch out of her mind.

He touched her elbow. "You okay? You seem distracted."

She looked down. "I'm fine. Nervous, but that's to be expected."

He tilted her head up. "I've been a good boy, Molly. We've played this your way. That's still what you want? Because I sure wouldn't have a problem with massaging away some of that tension." He smiled. "I think you'd be happy with the results."

"Brady, don't."

He dropped his hand. "Okay. It's business as usual. Four more days of practice and then you and the cowpoke be ready by noon on Thursday. I'll pick you up and take you to the airfield where Blake's plane will be waiting."

Molly resisted leaning into him and letting herself

be enclosed in his strong arms. Instead, she hugged her own arms around her chest. "We'll be ready."

"I've got plans tonight," he said. "But we'll pick up where we left off—poker-wise—tomorrow night."

"Fine." She watched him follow Shane into the barn, and tried to ignore the hollow feeling in the pit of stomach. He had plans tonight. She went up the stairs to the apartment. Yes, she definitely had to get Brady out of her mind. But how would she ever get him out of her heart? This man who had plans tonight had somehow found a place there and even Kevin seemed to be making room for him.

CHAPTER FIFTEEN

BRADY FOLLOWED MOLLY AND SAM onto the Learjet and whistled his appreciation. "Nice puddle-jumper you picked," he said to Blake who was making sure Annie was buckled in and comfortable in the first row.

"Glad you like it," Blake said. "I'm thinking Smith Industries should invest in one of these babies." He looked down the center aisle between the seats. "Maybe not a sixteen passenger, though. Something…"

Brady looked at Annie and finished his sentence for him. "Something just for the expanding immediate family?" he said.

"And a few close friends," Blake added.

Annie smiled, a pad and pencil in her hand. "Can I have a statement, Brady? How are you feeling at this moment?"

Brady rolled his eyes. "Tell me you're not here as a reporter, Annie."

"Hey, once a reporter… Anyway, the folks in River Bluff will want all the details."

Blake smiled. "You might as well talk to her, buddy. She won't give up."

"Okay," Brady said. "I'll give you a statement as soon as the tournament's over."

"Hey, Brady!"

He looked down the aisle. "What is it, Sam?"

The boy slid forward in his seat. "Look how cool this plane is. I've got a drink holder and everything! And Mom says there's even a bathroom in the back."

"I'll be right there to check it out, buckaroo," Brady said. He patted Blake's shoulder. "Thanks for arranging this."

"No problem. You nervous about the weekend?"

Hell, yes, he was, but not about poker. Over the past few days he'd found himself growing more and more anxious for Molly's sake. If she wanted to open that kids' store she'd been talking about, then he'd like to see her do it. Maybe he did owe her. That job at Cliff's Diner had been her livelihood. No matter how things worked out between them, he didn't want her to walk away with nothing. "Maybe a little."

"Vegas isn't going to tempt you back again with her bright lights and showgirls?"

"Not a chance," Brady said. "I got the message. High-stakes gambling isn't for me. I'm a horse trainer. It's what I want to be, maybe always has been."

Blake nodded his satisfaction with Brady's response and pointed to the back of the plane. "And I'm thinking your father agrees. I didn't figure he'd come along on this trip."

Brady waved to his parents. "Mom talked him into it. She really wanted to come." Brady didn't add that he was pleased to see his father taking Angela seriously. Those two had come a long way in the short time since Molly had been at Cross Fox. She'd done more than provide Brady with the chance to train a great horse. She'd made his mother feel needed again, especially to the man who, it turned out, needed her more than he realized.

"Just enjoy the ride, my friend," Blake said. "The one we've got ahead of us for two hours and the one you'll be on for the next three days."

"Will you two quit jabbering?" Luke snarled, jostling them with his elbows. "People are trying to get on the damn plane."

More back-slapping followed as the other members of the Wild Bunch, some with their partners, some without, boarded. The mood was jovial, expectant. And why not? It was a weekend in Vegas and for those who could bask in the lights of the strip and go home again, it was a fun experience. Brady was glad to be one of them.

Serafina and Dobbs sat across the aisle from Marshall and Angela. Dobbs, who claimed to be a seasoned flyer but who everyone knew was a white-knuckler, was explaining every prep noise to Serafina "in case she was nervous." She curled her hand over his and concentrated on her romance novel.

Molly sat next to Sam, letting him have the window seat. Brady sat across from them next to Colin Warner, who Brady now considered an honorary member of the Wild Bunch since turning him on to Amber Mac. Minutes after the seats filled, the jet surged over the tarmac and lifted into the sky as smooth as a filly on a dry track. When an attendant began serving drinks—as impossible as that seemed on such a small plane—Brady noticed his mother declined.

Then Jake leaned into the aisle and said in that commanding deep voice of his that couldn't be ignored, "Did everybody hear that Ed Falconetti has organized a caravan of cars to meet at the café tomorrow morning and head to Vegas?"

Molly looked at Brady anxiously. He'd heard but hadn't told her. Nor had he mentioned that since he'd entered the tournament the side bets at the restaurant had increased tremendously. Many of the bets favored Molly beating Brady at his own game. He'd taken a lot of good-natured ribbing from his neighbors about the outcome of this tournament.

"This is as exciting as when the Broncos went to the state high-school football finals," Marshall said. "Imagine, two people from River Bluff are going to be on TV, and a good percentage of our town will be in the cheering section."

Brady cringed. *Thanks, Dad.* Molly practically spilled her wine as she reached across the aisle and grabbed his arm. "TV?" she said. "I didn't know anything about this tournament being televised."

"I just heard myself," Brady admitted. "It's unusual to tape quarter finals, but Texas Hold 'Em has gotten that popular." Her grip tightened so he added, "But I wouldn't worry. It probably won't even make it on the air. There are more important tournaments to broadcast than this little one."

"I hope you're right." She mumbled something else—he thought he heard the word father. Interesting. She hadn't mentioned the man before. Figuring if she had something else to tell him she would, he didn't pursue the subject. Besides, from the way she'd just reacted, maybe avoiding the subject was best.

That would be easy for Brady. In fact, since his father had just referred to Molly as "one of River Bluff's own," he smiled. In the few weeks she'd been there, Molly had made an impression.

He couldn't help thinking about how great she'd look on TV though. The camera would love her. If the tournament promoters had gotten wind of the big bet, she might become one of the spotlight players. The event commentators could very well focus on Molly and him this weekend. A small-town waitress teaming up with a former Dallas Cowboy made a good story.

But Molly obviously wasn't going to like that, so he'd better hope he was wrong. Maybe nobody in the media even knew they were playing and their stay in Vegas wouldn't draw any attention.

An hour and a half later the plane landed and Brady and Molly walked out together. About a dozen people milled around on the tarmac. One of them spotted Brady and the rest closed in on him. When he and Molly reached the bottom step, at least a half dozen video cameras started rolling and as many microphones were shoved in their faces. Molly began to shake. Her face paled. For a moment Brady thought she was going to faint. He took her elbow and rushed her inside the terminal.

So much for anonymity.

MOLLY RAN INTO THE RESTROOM, which was conveniently located just inside the terminal door of the private landing facility. She heard Brady say as she went in, "I'll get rid of them, Molly, I promise."

Five minutes later she wondered if they were gone and how long she'd have to stay in the bathroom. And if she reacted this way today, what the heck was she going to do about television cameras at the tournament? She leaned on the sink and stared into the mirror. She looked tired, her skin drawn, her cheeks sallow. And the tournament hadn't even begun.

She shivered when her worst fear materialized in her mind. What would her father think if he happened to hear about his daughter gambling on TV? Worse, what if he saw her for himself? And did she really care?

Yes, she did. She and her father hadn't gotten along, but she never intended to hurt him.

"Molly? Honey, are you okay?"

Angela's image appeared in the mirror behind her. "I don't know," she said. "I didn't expect media."

Angela rested her hand on Molly's shoulder. "I know. It was a shock, but Brady sent them away. No one will bother you when you come out." She smiled. "And you do have to come out. Sam's starting to worry about you and I won't even go into how shaken Brady is. If we don't leave this bathroom, he's going to come in here. And I wouldn't be surprised if all those friends followed him."

The idea of River Bluff's Wild Bunch made Molly chuckle. Those five guys in the ladies' bathroom could cause quite a commotion. She stood straight, steeling herself for the inevitable. "For the sake of women who might need to use these facilities, I guess we'd better go out."

Angela was right. The reporters were gone. The only people waiting outside were the ones from the plane. And they immediately surrounded Molly.

"You all right?" Luke asked.

Sam grabbed her hand. "Yeah, Mom, are you okay?"

Jake shook his head. "Those stupid reporters. It was obvious you were upset. I've got half a mind—"

Annie held up her hands and waved them back. "Will you guys just step away and let the woman catch her breath?"

Molly smiled her gratitude and ruffled Sam's hair. "Of course I'm okay, Sam. I'm fine." She stared pointedly at Brady's friends. "Just had to use the restroom."

"That's what Brady said, but I didn't believe him," Sam said.

Brady leaned in close and whispered, "Camera-shy, are you?"

"Not ordinarily. And not if it's just one camera at a time… Did you know to expect this?"

"To this degree? Honestly, Molly, I didn't."

"How did the reporters even know anything? They certainly weren't here to see me, and you only decided to play a few days ago."

"I asked one of them that. He said a tournament official happened to see my name on the list and word got out. Then someone in the media talked to somebody in River Bluff and found out about the wager."

"I'll bet it was Ed," Jake said. "He'd do anything to get publicity for the café."

"Could have been," Brady admitted. "Anyway, I guess it's considered news now, human-interest stuff anyway."

"But our flight?" Molly said. "It was a private plane. How did they know when you would arrive?"

"Flight plans aren't secret, Molly. Not too many Learjets take off from a private airstrip in River Bluff bound for Las Vegas."

She nodded. "I guess not."

"Promise me you won't let the attention break your concentration," he said. "I'll give the media a statement, explain about the bet and minimize its significance. That should be the end of it. I'll try to keep the focus off you, so it won't be too bad."

Molly found her overnight bag among their suitcases and looped it over her shoulder. If only I could believe that, she thought. But any coverage at all with her name in it would cause a major problem with her dad.

Brady led her toward the terminal exit. "We don't have to be in the poker room until ten o'clock tomorrow. Tonight's just for sightseeing. I guarantee that the strip will make you forget about reporters."

"Yeah, Mom," Sam said, his eyes darting from one glamorous showgirl poster to the next as they proceeded to the door. "We're gonna have a blast tonight."

"Sure we will, Sammy."

MARSHALL PICKED UP THE TAB for everyone associated with Cross Fox Ranch at the hotel café the next morning. "I guess this is it," he said to Brady and Molly. "Good luck. May the better woman win."

Brady laughed. "Funny, Dad. And she just might."

Angela gave Molly a kiss on the cheek. "Don't be nervous. Look at this as one of life's adventures." She drew Molly aside and said, "Speaking for myself, win or lose, you and Sam can stay at Cross Fox as long as you like. And I know Serafina doesn't want to lose you as a bookkeeper, so try to enjoy yourself over these next two days. There's no pressure for you to leave us."

Molly appreciated Angela's kindness, but she knew that once the tournament was over, she and Sam would go. "Thanks, Angela. Despite the butterflies in my stomach, I think I'm ready. Your son has been a thorough teacher. I just hope I remember all the statistics and strategies he's drummed into me."

"You'll do fine." She tapped the side of Molly's head. "Remember, it's not just what's up here that counts. Luck is important, too, and we can't control that factor."

"Luck, skill, concentration, instinct…" Molly laughed. "At this point, I don't know what counts most."

Angela looped her hand through Marshall's elbow. "Fun is what's important. So have some." She smiled up at her husband. "That's what we intend to do, right, honey?"

"Absolutely. But we'll check back on you kids in a while." He looked down at Sam. "So what do you say, Sam, my boy. You ready to see some Vegas exhibits?"

"You bet I am." He waved at Molly. "Good luck, Mom. See you later."

"Right. Be a good boy for Mr. and Mrs. Carrick."

Within seconds Sam and the others had disappeared into the crowd, leaving only Molly and Brady to head toward the casino poker room. "What are your friends doing today?" she asked.

"I heard the girls say they were going to split their time between the slots and the pool. The guys you can probably guess. They'll spend the better part of the day at the tables. But they've all promised to come to the poker room later this afternoon to see if we've survived. If we have, then they'll all be in the spectator section tomorrow when it really counts."

"How should you and I act toward each other?" Molly asked. "Should we pretend we don't know each other?"

"Heck, no. Just be yourself. Many of the players are acquainted with each other. Poker's gotten popular, but it's still a small world where everyone recognizes everyone else. A lot of the contestants today will have competed many times."

"I suppose it'll be cutthroat in there among the professional players."

"Not necessarily. You'll see some pros, but mostly guys like me who just love the game and a lot of amateurs like you trying their luck. It's a fairly easygoing atmosphere until the second day when things heat up."

Once they passed through the slot machines, they were in a huge room filled with poker tables enclosed by a decorative wood fence. A casino official stood at the entrance beside a sign that said the area was reserved for the next two days for the U.S. Poker Play-offs.

For an instant Molly stopped breathing. She didn't know what she'd expected. Certainly nothing like this mammoth space. And, she realized immediately, at least ninety percent of the players were men.

"Impressive, isn't it?" Brady said.

Her voice quaked as she said, "That's one word for it."

He walked up to the man in charge. "I'm Brady Carrick."

"I recognize you, Mr. Carrick," the official said. "We've been expecting you and we're delighted you decided to enter this season's event." He smiled.

"And this must be Miss Davis, the poker whiz everyone's been telling me about."

Molly's heart thundered, practically drowning out the man's voice. She clutched Brady.

He patted her hand reassuringly. "This is Molly," he said.

The official handed him two sets of papers. "You'll find your first table assignments in here, as well as our no-limit tournament rules. If you have any questions, feel free to ask me before we get started."

"Thank you." Brady took the papers. "We have a while until play begins," he said to Molly. "Let's find a quiet corner and go over everything."

Too numb to answer, Molly nodded. Still dazed by the enormity of what she'd gotten herself into, she let Brady take her to a plush bench in the casino lobby. He handed her the rules and went over them one by one. "It's standard stuff, Mol," he assured her. "You already know all this from playing those tournaments in Grand Pass."

She exhaled deeply and stared at him. "I'm in over my head, Brady. Way over. Is there any way you can get your thousand dollars back and I can go out to the pool with Annie?"

He grinned. "Nope. And I don't want to. You're going to win that much and a whole lot more. Remember, there are five hundred people starting out today. You only have to be in the top seventy-five to have a winning payday."

His gaze lowered from her face to her chest. Her

heart skipped when he reached out and picked up the turquoise pendant. His knuckles brushed her bare skin above the V neckline of her sweater. "Besides, sweetheart, you have your lucky charm. What can go wrong?"

Instinctively, she wrapped her hand around his. She'd long ago stopped thinking of Kevin's gift as lucky, but with Brady's warm grasp circling the talisman today, she thought that perhaps it might be. Except now she was having doubts that she wanted to be lucky enough to beat him. Her eyes welled up. She tried to smile. "Thanks."

He helped her to her feet and they returned to the poker room. Two minutes later, with a stack of chips in front of her, she sat between two men, one middle-aged and well-groomed in a business suit, the other, Asian with so much gold around his neck she wondered how he could hold his head up. She ordered iced tea from a waitress, before she saw a man with a camera in a far corner of the room. She was certain the lens rotated toward her. And then two cards were dealt face down in front of her. She stole a peek at a pair of queens and began playing poker.

AT EIGHT O'CLOCK that night, three tables had to be pulled together at the hotel steak house to accommodate everyone who'd flown into town on Blake's plane. Luke offered to pay for the first round and nobody denied him the pleasure. Finally relaxed after the long day, Molly said, "I'll say one thing for the Wild Bunch. You guys know how to party."

Brady raised his glass. "Especially when we've got something to celebrate."

"Has anybody heard from Ed and the rest of the group driving in?" Jake asked.

No one had, but ten minutes later, Brady's cell phone rang. He checked the caller ID screen. "Speak of the devil. That's Falconetti now." He hit the connect button. "What's up, Ed?"

He covered the speaker grid and spoke to the group. "They got here a couple of hours ago."

"How many came?" Marshall wanted to know.

"Twenty people," Brady told him.

"Where are they?" Cole asked.

Brady repeated the question to Ed. "They're all standing outside Treasure Island watching the pirate show."

"Figures that's where Ed would be," Luke said. "That's free."

Brady waited for the laughter to die down and asked Ed to repeat his last question.

"So is one of you still in the tournament?" Ed said. "Or did we drive all the way up here just for a rollicking good time?"

"Believe it or not, we're both still in," Brady said. "Out of the original five hundred players, two hundred are left, each of us hoping to eventually be in the top seventy-five."

"What time do you start in the morning?" Ed asked.

"Ten o'clock."

"Whoa. That's early. We'll drop by at noon to see how you're doing. If either you or Molly are still playing, we'll stick around to provide a few Bronx cheers."

Brady smiled. Ed was the one who could do it.

After dinner, Brady was talked into hitting the craps tables. "Want to come, Molly? A lady shooter is good luck."

She looked down at Sam who could barely keep his eyes open. "I don't think so. This party boy's got to get some shut-eye, right, Sammy?"

He laid his head against Molly's hip. "No argument?" Brady said. "I guess he's really wrung out. Meet for breakfast at nine, Molly?"

"Sure, that'll be fine. See you then."

She walked toward the bank of elevators. Brady resisted a sudden urge to follow her. She had a small suite on the twelfth floor. Sam could go to bed in one room and he and Molly could sit in front of the TV and…

He shook his head, but the image of Molly nestled in his arms, her head on his shoulder wouldn't go away. He was proud of the way she'd played today. She'd stayed focused, relied on good instincts to make the right decisions. She'd wowed everybody in the room. And him. But watching her now, Brady knew it wasn't his pride that made him want to be alone with her tonight. Nope, it wasn't pride at all. What he was feeling for Molly was something much more serious.

"Hey, Molly?" he called after her.

She turned around.

"Only a hundred and twenty-five players to go before we're guaranteed to be in the winner's column. We going to do it?"

She gave him two thumbs-up. "I can see the finish line from here, just like Amber Mac sprinting on a fast track."

He smiled as he watched her walk away. For a moment his heart stopped. It was the moment he realized he loved her.

SKILL. Luck. Talent. Determination. They all combined the next day to keep Molly and Brady alive in the tournament. One by one, the remaining twenty-three tables of nine players were whittled down as more contestants threw their losing cards on the felt and went to the "pink lady," the casino official, who handed them their tournament placement cards.

At five o'clock, only six players remained. All of them were guaranteed to take home significant winnings. One of them would have their entry to the semifinals paid for. And Molly and Brady were among them. The six players were each interviewed on camera. Molly resisted, but in the end she said a few words to the personable female commentator who complimented her success and asked about her strategy. She credited the River Bluff crowd for supporting her all the way with applause for good hands and encouragement for bad ones.

The tournament director gathered the six players together, went over a few essential rules for the last round of play and told them to be back in one hour for the showdown. He didn't need to, but he reminded them that a thirty-thousand-dollar grand prize was at stake.

"I'm going to my room," Molly said when the group broke up. "I'll get Sam from Serafina's room and order in a couple of sandwiches."

"Is it okay if I join you?" Brady asked.

"Sure. We're friendly competitors."

"I'll be up there in a few minutes after I let the guys know."

She walked away. He spoke to his friends and was assured they would be present for the last round. Then he went to find Molly. He rounded a corner and realized she hadn't gone up in the elevators yet. She was talking to someone he didn't recognize. And she didn't look happy.

As Brady walked closer, he heard the man's angry voice spouting something about a church secretary seeing an article in the local paper. The man shook his finger in Molly's face. "She'll tell everyone in town," he said. "If you don't care about your reputation, at least think about what your actions are doing to me."

The man was older, gray-haired, thin and several inches shorter than Brady. But he was definitely a threat. He reached out and gripped Molly's arm. Adrenaline spiked in Brady's bloodstream and he quickly closed the distance between them, yanking on the man's wrist, forcing him to release her. "What the hell do you think you're doing?" he said.

Molly's eyes registered her shock. "It's okay, Brady. It's nothing."

The man turned his irate gaze on Brady. "Young man, let go of me right now. I'm trying to talk some sense into her."

Brady wasn't about to let go. The man was clearly agitated. "How about if I take you to security instead," Brady said.

"No!" Molly tried to step between them. "Leave it be, Brady. This is none of your concern."

"The hell it isn't."

"I would expect such language from you, Brady Carrick," the man said.

Brady's heart kicked into a full gallop. This guy knew his last name. Was he a poker fan? A Cowboys fan? Brady didn't think so. "Yeah? Well, would you also expect a punch in the face? Because that's what you're about to get."

Molly tugged on Brady's arm. "Don't hit him. Please, Brady. Let it go."

Confusion warred with Brady's escalating anger. What was going on? Why was Molly defending this Neanderthal? Brady looked in the man's eyes. They blazed with righteous indignation, but they were clear. No sign of a drunken haze. "Who are you?" Brady demanded.

"I'm her father, that's who I am. Pastor Luther Whelan from Prairie Bend, Texas."

Brady dropped his hand. "Her father?"

"And I don't need to ask who you are." He glared at Molly, pointed in her face again and said, "What you two are doing is sinful. You're playing the devil's games and he'll take you down."

Molly seemed to shrink before Brady's eyes. She stared at the circle of onlookers who'd gathered around them. She clutched the turquoise charm with a trembling hand. "Go away, Dad," she said. "Please, just go away."

"I'll go, gladly, if you do the right thing and come with me. I only want to save you and my grandson." As violent as he'd been, the man changed, lowered his voice as if his anger was suddenly spent. "I've missed you," he said.

Molly bit her lip. "I'm sorry, Dad, but I'm not leaving here. We'll talk when this is over. I promise."

Whelan leaned close to her. Every muscle in Brady's body tensed again. "If you stay here, you're lost," Whelan said. "There is only one choice to make."

She squared her shoulders and spoke with unbelievable calm. "Then I choose lost, Dad." Her expression as sad as any he'd ever seen, she looked at Brady and said, "Promise me you won't hurt him."

Reeling from his own shock, Brady managed to nod.

"Thank you." She turned away from them and, with as much dignity as she could muster, she entered a waiting elevator.

Whelan turned on Brady. "This is all your doing. You brought her here. You tempted her with riches, blinded her to her faith and her responsibilities."

Brady held his hands up. "I didn't tempt her to do anything. You've just seen that she has a mind of her own."

The pastor went on as if Brady hadn't spoken. "It wasn't enough that you took her husband away from her. You couldn't stop there."

Brady struggled to grasp what the man was talking about. "Took her husband?"

"Kevin Davis. Remember him? A luckless, godless rodeo cowboy."

Brady felt as if he'd been punched. All the air rushed from his lungs. The stubborn bull rider? His name was Kevin. Brady remembered it as clearly as if it had happened yesterday. He pictured the brash young cowboy reaching over the bar, introducing himself, bragging about his exploits that day. It all came back with the same agonizing regret. Kevin's body on the sidewalk.

Brady's voice shook. "Molly was married to him?"

"That's right. To the man you dragged into your web of gambling and women."

"It wasn't like that."

Whelan continued, his anger mounting again. "I despised Kevin. He was a worthless provider and a man of many weaknesses. Which is why someone like you, with your wealth, influence and reputation could destroy him. Because that's what you did,

Brady Carrick, as surely as if you'd pushed him off that roof." His voice shook. "And now you want to destroy my daughter by taking her away from me."

CHAPTER SIXTEEN

BRADY PUSHED HIS WAY past Whelan and headed for the elevators. Though his thoughts tumbled wildly, his only goal now was to get to Molly.

Molly, married to Kevin. She had to know what her husband had been doing the night he died and she had to know Brady had been there. Perhaps fate had intervened when Brady met her at the diner in Prairie Bend, but he suspected that everything that happened since then had been carefully planned.

She'd kept the truth from him. All those questions he'd asked her about her husband. Her evasive answers. Damn. Brady had even called the guy a jerk. Cruel in hindsight, but he hadn't known. So why hadn't Molly told him the connection? What did she hope to gain? Did the woman he loved hate him? He couldn't believe that. Her kisses said otherwise.

He punched the up elevator button, stared at the directional arrows on the wall, waiting… Did Molly blame him for what happened to her husband? He had no way of knowing what she and Kevin talked about the night he died, or if they talked at all.

Pieces of conversations came back to Brady now and he began to see his relationship with Molly in a clear light. Her tightly wound emotions, her subtle criticisms, her defense of Sam. Everything started to make a crazy kind of sense. *But she doesn't know my side of the story,* Brady thought. She'd never given him a chance to explain. If she believed half of what her father did, she must think Brady the most despicable man in all of Texas. Hell, he'd almost thought that himself.

The doors opened. Brady rushed inside, hit the button to the twelfth floor. What was he going to do when he got to her room? Should he apologize? Wait for her to? He'd never deceived her. Never mind whose mistakes were worse. Right now all he cared about was knowing that she was okay.

He practically ran down the hall. "Molly, it's me," he called, pounding on her door.

Nothing. He listened for voices.

"I know you're in there," he called. "Open up."

Nothing. He hit the door with the side of his fist. "Let me in, Molly, or I swear, I'll break this door down."

God, what was happening to him? He didn't act this way around women. Hell, he didn't act this crazy around anybody. He didn't threaten to do stupid, macho things. That's why he'd been so successful on the football field. He'd channeled any frustrations he felt in real life into the game. Now his aggression was directed at a damn door.

He took a deep breath. "Molly, please open up. We need to talk."

He waited, counting to keep his emotions in check. He'd reached nine when the door slowly pulled back a few inches. She stood there, her eyes shimmering, her lips trembling. "You know?"

More relieved than he'd ever felt in his life, he attempted to smile. "Your father isn't very good at subtlety." He tried to see inside. "Is Sam in here with you?"

She shook her head.

"Good. Then let me in. I need to tell you what happened that night."

She opened the door all the way, let him in and closed and locked it. "I know what happened, Brady. I talked to Kevin before—" Her voice caught. "I know he was drunk when he met you and I know what he was like when he was that way. He had some money. He probably told you he did."

"He recognized me in the bar and we started talking," Brady explained. "He was proud of his win that day."

She walked over to the window which looked out onto the lights of the strip. "I'm sure he was an easy mark for you and your friends."

Brady couldn't deny it. Kevin had been like hundreds of drifters who came to Vegas hoping to score with a few bucks in their pockets. He *was* an easy mark. He made himself one.

He walked toward her, but stopped when he saw her stiffen. "I didn't encourage him to play, Molly. I swear. I knew he'd be in over his head."

"That's not the way he told the story to me on the telephone," she said. "Anyway, you allowed him to get in that game. That's just as bad. You knew he was drunk. You took advantage of a man who saw the great Brady Carrick and wanted to be part of his circle for one night." She lowered her face. He saw her sad reflection in the window. "He idolized you, Brady. Did you know that? He never missed a Cowboys' game."

"That's not the impression I got when I met him. In that bar, I knew what he wanted and that was to beat me. He didn't want to be my friend, Molly. He wanted to be the one who took me down—which is kind of ironic. At that time in my life, I didn't have very far to fall."

She wiped a tear from her cheek and turned to face him. "Here's the real irony, Brady. You took *him* down. You played a poor drunken cowboy for all he was worth. You and your friends took his money and his dignity."

Brady looked at the ceiling. God, how he'd tried to warn Kevin. All through the game, he'd kept telling him to quit, to go back to his motel. But the guy wouldn't stop. He kept tossing in money until it was gone.

"You stole his pride," Molly said, her voice trembling "When he jumped from that roof, he wasn't the man I married. The man I married would have come home to me." She walked to the sofa, picked up her purse and unzipped an inside compartment. She withdrew some bills and held them up to Brady's eyes. "See these? Three one-hundred-dollar bills." She crumpled them in her fist and threw them at Brady. They hit his chest and landed on the carpet. "That's what the police sent me along with Kevin's clothes. Three hundred dollars—all I had left from ten years of marriage."

He stared at her before lowering his gaze to the money. This was incredible. He knew where those bills had come from. He remembered putting them in Kevin's pocket when he told him to go home. To ease his guilt. Molly had kept them all this time. A symbol of her hate.

She pointed to the money. "Pick them up, Brady. You might as well have the rest of Kevin's money and finish the job."

For a moment he thought she might collapse. He reached out his hand. She ignored it and sat heavily on the sofa. Her shoulders sagged. She took a deep breath as if her anger had suddenly ebbed. "No matter what," she said, "he always came home to me. Somehow I always put us back together again. But not this time."

Brady knelt before her. His knee popped, and pain shot up his thigh. He ignored it. "I told him to leave, Molly. Over and over. I begged him."

"He was drunk!" she said again as if that explained everything, made Brady's sin even worse. "He didn't know what he was doing. You could have stopped him before he ever got in that game. You're the great Brady Carrick!"

"No…" he paused, and suddenly remembered the one thing that might redeem him in Molly's eyes. When he offered to buy Kevin a beer that night in the bar, Kevin said he was finishing off his first one of the day. He accepted Brady's offer because he was celebrating. Brady looked into Molly's eyes. "Listen to me, Molly. This is the truth. Kevin wasn't drunk when I met him in the Mirage bar. He'd had one beer."

"I talked to him. I know…"

"Molly, he was sober! He wanted in that game, but it wasn't liquor talking. It was him. He might have been high on a rodeo win, but I swear, he wasn't high on booze when he made the decision to play. He was a guy with money in his pocket and the confidence of a big win in his gut and he made a bad decision that night."

Brady suddenly realized that what his friends had been telling him all these months was true. He wasn't responsible for what Kevin did that night. He wasn't to blame for another man's mistakes. He regretted what happened to that cowboy. He always would. But on that night, they were each making decisions that would affect them in monumental ways. That poker game signified an end for each of them. Only Kevin didn't go home and Brady did.

He placed his hands on Molly's knees. "You have to believe me, Molly. I'm telling you the truth. I'm as sorry as I can be about what happened to Kevin, what you and Sam had to face…your grief. But Kevin made his own choices that night."

She stared at him, tears running down her cheeks.

And the familiar phrase came back to him. *If I'd only…* But the awful guilt that had accompanied that phrase no longer weighed him down, because Brady hoped that something good would come from all this heartache. And he realized that something good already had. Molly had left the stifling environment of her father's influence and refused to go back. Her son had made strides toward becoming a happy, well-adjusted kid. And just maybe she would see in Brady what he saw in her. The goodness, the compassion, the love.

"Do you believe me, Mol?" He waited. She wiped her face. "I've just asked you the most important question I've ever asked anyone in my life," he said. "Your answer matters, more than you can know." He took her hands, one in each of his. "Do you believe me when I tell you how it was that night?"

THROUGH THE BLUR of her tears Molly stared at his face. She couldn't just say yes, could she? After all these months of searching for a way to mend the rip in her heart that she believed Brady had torn, could she simply cast all the animosity aside and say the words he wanted to hear?

It was Brady's hand clasping hers now, not Kevin's. His hold was warm, comforting, strong. Kevin had been everything to her, the one who'd allowed her to forget where she'd come from. With Kevin it didn't matter that her past had been filled with sin and self-recrimination. But it was Brady who was here, holding her, his comfort constant and soothing, his presence profound.

She sniffed, pushed her hair back from her forehead. Brady waited on his knees. When he winced, she knew he was hurting. "Get up," she said, struggling with a smile.

"Not until you say you believe me."

She patted the sofa beside her. "I believe you."

He released a ragged rush of air and sat. "Thanks. My leg was beginning to stiffen up."

"I know." Fresh tears stung her eyes. Brady brushed them away.

"Believing is just the beginning, Molly," he said. "I've forgiven myself for what happened that night. It didn't come easy, but I've finally accepted that I did all I could to stop Kevin. I need to know that you forgive me, too."

He tucked a strand of her hair behind her ear and laid his hand on her shoulder. She blinked his face into focus and suddenly knew a truth that she had denied for too long. It wasn't Brady she had to forgive. It was Kevin. He had let her down by committing the ultimate betrayal. And the promises he'd made to her and Sam over the years died with him.

She sighed, felt her tense muscles relax. Why had she been so stupid before? She laid her hand against Brady's cheek. He needed a shave. The roughness of his five o'clock shadow made him real, vital and very dear. "You're not the person I need to forgive," she said.

"What do you mean?"

She let Kevin go for now. He didn't belong in this

moment. "The person who most needs my forgiveness is myself."

His brow furrowed. "That's crazy, Mol. What do you have to forgive yourself for?"

Molly took the biggest gamble she'd ever taken in her life. Even bigger than when she packed up her belongings and left Prairie Bend with her seven-year-old son. She stared hard at the man who held her hand as if he'd never let go and whose bristling beard scraped her palm. "I need to forgive myself for loving you more than I ever loved Kevin."

He squeezed her hand tightly. She hoped that meant he felt the same. The words were out there now. She couldn't take them back and despite what the future might hold from this point forward, she didn't want to. Her admission had been cleansing, strangely like the fulfilling of a prophecy that had begun in the parking lot of a dusty north Texas diner. Pastor Whelan's daughter smiled and thought, *damn the consequences.*

Brady shifted on the sofa to face her squarely. Then he let go of her hand and opened his arms. "Molly, my darlin', come here."

And she did.

THE KISS was everything Molly had wished for. At first sweet, full of promise. Then demanding, passionate and, thank goodness, life-altering. She'd never been kissed like this before and all she could think about was being kissed like this for the rest of her life.

At a knock on the door, Brady reluctantly pulled away from her. "Who's there?" he hollered.

"Mom? What are you doing?"

Molly giggled, a bright, cheery sound that seemed foreign to her yet comfortable. "We'd better stop."

"Son?" Marshall said. "You in there? Time's wasting. You've got to be downstairs."

Brady pressed his finger over her lips. "Shh. We'll pretend we didn't hear them."

"We can't do that. We're supposed to be playing poker in a few minutes. The final round."

"Oh, right." He stood, smoothed his shirtfront. "Hang on a minute, Dad. We'll be right there." Reaching out his hand, he pulled Molly up from the sofa. "You want to skip it?"

"Do you think we could?" He shrugged, and she realized he was close to blowing off the tournament. "We can't," she said. "All your friends are here. And our neighbors." *Our* neighbors. It sounded nice, like she belonged somewhere. She pointed to the door. "Your father. Sam."

"Okay. We'll play." He kissed her quickly and started for the door. "But I don't give a fly on a goat's heinie who wins."

The urge to beat Brady had disappeared along with the urge to play poker at all, but they were obligated. "I do," she said. "I care who wins."

"Yeah? You still want to take home the big check?"

She smiled. "No. I'm kind of rooting for that old gentleman who came all the way from Tennessee. He told me it's been his lifelong ambition to play a tournament in Vegas. I want him to win."

Brady turned the dead bolt on the door, looked over his shoulder. "It's a good thing you're pulling for him, because my mind's not on poker." He winked at her. "Besides, we've won enough to open a shop in River Bluff."

Sam rushed in the door followed by Marshall and Angela. Serafina and Dobbs waited in the hall. "What's going on in here?" Marshall asked. "You're about to miss the final round."

Brady waited for Molly to pick up her purse. "None of your business and we're on our way."

Angela laughed at the shock on Marshall's face. "Some things really aren't your business, honey," she said.

"Wait, Mom!" Sam had squatted on the floor. He held up the crumpled bills. "Look at all this money. Can I have it?"

Molly stopped, looked at Brady, then down at Sam. "Yes, you can," she said. "That money is a gift from your daddy. I've saved it for you all this time, and when we get back home, we're going to open a savings account for your college education. What do you say to that?"

"I'd rather have an Xbox. There's this kid at school…"

Molly took the money, stuffed it in her purse. "We'll talk about that later."

"Come on, cowboy." Brady wrapped one arm around Sam and the other around Molly. As he passed Dobbs, he said loud enough for his father to hear, "Thanks for all that horse sense you've given me over the years, Dobbs. But look out. I'm gunning for your job."

Marshall laughed. "And now, with Molly getting to the final table, you've got training rights to the horse that'll help you get it."

And a whole lot more. Brady squeezed Molly's shoulder and looked down the hall. Heading toward them were four of the finest men he'd ever known.

"We've been looking all over for you," Luke said.

"Hurry up, B.C.!" Jake yelled. "You'll be late."

Cole and Blake gestured wildly at the elevators.

"Hold your horses," Brady said. "We're coming."

His dad was right. He had the horse that could define his future. And the best damn posse in the state of Texas at the end of the hallway. And now he had the woman of his heart and a family. He smiled. He'd never made a surer bet than the one he made in Prairie Bend. What happened downstairs tonight didn't make a lick of difference. Suddenly it wasn't all about the game. It was about life, and fate had dealt him a winning hand.

EPILOGUE

THE GENTLEMAN FROM TENNESSEE won the quarter finals. But when Molly and Brady boarded the plane for the flight back to River Bluff, they knew who the real winners were.

* * * * *

Don't miss the Wild Bunch heroes
when they deal out their Texas Hold 'Em hands
again next month—because the buck stops here.
Look for Luke's story TEXAS BLUFF
by Linda Warren in February 2008,
wherever Harlequin books are sold.
Turn the page for a sneak peek....

P- M M M - 3
K A D - 5
D
K

C+D - 2

W - R - L - K - W
D
GK A|M B T H C W A

7
14
2

"I DON'T KNOW, Bec." Luke crossed his arms over his chest. "When I was going down in the Hawk, I was pretty sure death was knocking at my door. I had these flashes of my life in my head and most every other frame was your face. My one thought as the chopper hit the ground was I'm going to die and Becky will never know how sorry I am for all the hurt I caused her."

Becky swallowed and wrapped her arms around her waist against the chill of the night breeze. But it wasn't just the night that sent the chill through her. It was his words. For sixteen years she'd been avoiding this conversation. Now she had to face the truth.

"Luke, we have to move on."

"That's what I'm trying to do." He crossed one booted ankle over the other. "But to put the past behind me I have to know that you forgive me for being a stupid teenage boy."

She bit her trembling lip.

"Sixteen years is a long time, but what we had back then was powerful and real. I'm the one who screwed up. I take the blame and I'm not angry at Rachel or you. I just want to move forward with my own life."

Oh God, she felt like bawling, and she didn't know why. Maybe it was fear. Maybe it was the thought of finally saying goodbye to their teenage romance. Because that's exactly what she had to do.

For both of them.

"I forgive you, Luke." The words came from deep within her heart, where they'd been buried for so many years.

He didn't say anything, but she felt his eyes on her and she rushed into speech. "I'm sorry it took me so long to say that. Back then I was every boy's friend. I helped with their homework, loaned them paper, pens and notebooks. I was the first one they called to find out if so-and-so was interested in them. Not once did any of them ask me to go for a burger or to the movies. I know a lot of that had to do with my father."

"It had everything to do with your father."

"I know, and then Luke Chisum asked me out. I couldn't believe it and I never stopped to ask why. I was so excited because I'd had a crush on you since eighth grade."

"Really?"

"Yeah. And when I found out the truth, I was devastated. I couldn't get beyond all that pain and humiliation."

"Bec..."

"It's okay, Luke. I finally understand what happened. I was just hurt too deeply to listen."

"I'm sorry I hurt you."

"And I'm sorry it took me so long to get to this point. But I'm truly over the past."

He straightened and touched the back of his fingers to her cheek. "Thanks, Becky. That's all I needed to hear."

Her cheek burned from his touch and soft lingering memories floated around her. She was glad the darkness hid the expression in her eyes.

"Goodbye, Becky," he said, sliding a long leg into his truck.

"'Night, Luke." For some reason she couldn't say goodbye. Maybe because she'd said goodbye to Luke a long time ago.

She turned and headed back to the house.

Coward, coward, echoed in her head. She hadn't told Luke everything. And she should have.